· *Fluffy Butch* ·

At fourteen, Mary had watched the half-naked, bell-bottomed men with a dizzy crush. They challenged her conservative, modest thighs with gentle voices and tambourines. With Heather, Mary wasn't just attracted to a woman, she was attracted to a woman who reminded her of her dream man. For a girl with simple tastes, Mary was about to complicate the whole show.

Eda Zahl grew up in the *National Geographic* magazine, travelling and posing for pictures for her father's yearly articles on natural phenomena. She graduated from Bennington College, worked on Broadway as an actress, and moved to Los Angeles, where she now lives and works full time as a writer.

· *Eda Zahl* ·

Fluffy
Butch

Mandarin

A Mandarin Paperback
FLUFFY BUTCH

First published in Great Britain 1994
by Mandarin Paperbacks
an imprint of Reed Consumer Books Ltd
Michelin House, 81 Fulham Road, London SW3 6RB
and Auckland, Melbourne, Singapore and Toronto

Copyright © Eda Zahl 1994
the author has asserted her moral rights

A CIP catalogue record for this title
is available from the British Library
ISBN 0 7493 1747 7

Printed and bound in Great Britain
by Cox & Wyman Ltd, Reading, Berks

To Joe Cappelli

· *One* ·

Mary learned to love men when she started dating women. She started dating women for two reasons. One was lust, lying dormant, until the legendary lover's kiss released its force. The other reason which fuelled the lust was that Mary was fed up.

The sublime connection, the male and female, for which we leave the mothers and fathers who love us had become too hard for her. The grim reports from the sexual battleground indicated that surrender led mainly to dominance, misunderstanding and rage. There were no romantic movies anymore to bolster her spirits when Oprah, Phil and Geraldo showed her daily the ugly alliances requiring a doctor's care and a library of books to determine who does the dishes. Being in love was not politically correct.

Still the promise of a tender match lingered until Time Magazine announced that women over thirty-five had a better chance of being hit by lightning than finding a mate. Soon Mary stopped looking at men. Too easily influenced, she became a media victim. The blindness crept up on her. First she stopped seeing the successful ones; the boys driving the black Porsches with the car phones. They drove too fast and fucked too fast. Then the intellectual ones faded. They feigned interest in her poems, but all they really wanted was a girl with big breasts. The third world exotics were fun for a night, but they needed a green card. Then the workers disappeared from sight. Either she was too busy working or they were too busy working. The cute guys were the last to go, but even their radiant smiling confidence stopped being a distraction. Finally, all the men were invisible.

Mary wished she could quietly absorb the gender panic that was in the air, but she wasn't comfortable with ambiguity. Even too many clothes in her wardrobe gave her too much choice. By eliminating a sex, and all patterned clothing, she hoped her life would become simpler and easier.

Like the feral creatures that pretend invisibility by standing rock still when the hunter approaches, only to be killed by an easy shot, Mary assumed that if she didn't see men, they wouldn't see her. This plan didn't work. She was thirty-five, but she still looked good enough, even if she did wear only two colours, black and grey. The male barrage of compliments, covert superiority and attraction didn't stop.

There was only one way to end it, and by ending it, she might fall in love with the enemy. Mary was going to find out first-hand what it takes to be a man. Like Dr Jekyll, the true scientist, Mary knew the only real information would come from experimenting on herself. And like Dr Jekyll again, she had no idea how strong Mr Hyde could become when given his voice. Her curiosity, will and exceptionally beautiful hair were the only qualities that separated Mary from the rest of the tired women, and she finally called off the whole game when she shaved her head; a single, drastic action that made the world react to her in a brand new way. She didn't see them, but Lawrence, Jimmy and Arthur saw her and fought for Mary while Mary fought for Heather, Joanne and Debra. In this confusion lies Mary's story.

Bald Mary moved to Los Angeles alone. She'd read that women outnumber men eight to one in the glamorous media capital. This statistic, the weather and Hollywood made it a perfect spot in her opinion. But Los Angeles is a big city, bigger than anybody but the natives realise, and Mary got lost. With no one to read her Eastern characteristics, so recognisable in New York, D.C. and Boston, she floundered. Parts of her identity existed only in reflected light. And the haircut, cute as it was on St Joan, in Mary's case further obscured her gender, education, and the simplest visual clues that reveal background and attract sympathetic friends.

Without significant hair, the normal world didn't see her. Even a cute razor cut, with its spikes and tails, would have signalled rebellion, yes, but remained safe and reassuring in it's trendiness and fashionable female anger. On the other hand, real midnight scissor cuts showing actual scalp pushed her out of the neighbourhoods and networks she'd always used. Landlords ignored a strong credit history and gave apartments to someone else. Interviews for good jobs in her field of marketing research were immediately terminated with abrupt manufactured excuses. One personnel executive actually faked sudden illness before Mary had time to sit down and give him her résumé. Salespeople got very busy, and her uncle in Sherman Oaks with a spare bedroom over the garage looked so disappointed and shaken by his ex-frilly niece that Mary moved out. It was her first winter in the city, and fifty degrees in a halter top felt cold. She was still dressing like a tourist.

Eventually she found a halfway house in the middle of a bad neighbourhood. On one side of the street, a few ancient hookers flagged down uninsured Pontiacs with their doors painted a different colour to their bodies. On the other side of the street, some Mexicans, without machismo, sold dope. To call them dealers would be too dignified. They were selling a few pills and a little cut blow, probably stolen from the hookers.

Mary liked living in the house with the street girls. Most of them were gay. Mary wasn't sure why but she felt comfortable with these women. Sitting on the Goodwill furniture, and listening to DeBarge, she watched the girls sort of dance by themselves until bedtime. They said hi, but didn't expect talk or even a smile, which was such a relief. They seemed to know about not having the energy or desire to smile. The nightly slabs of homemade chocolate sheet cake running with fat and glaze from industrial tubs of margarine and sugar helped lift everyone's spirits, but the trade-off was bad skin which depressed everybody again. The girl assigned to baking the cakes was a heroin addict and her idea of proportion leaned to excess. When dessert came, the housemates braced their jaws for that first bite where they could feel the sugar still granular in the icing that instantly opened every salivating gland and jolted their brains into momentary alertness and fellowship.

The social workers organized rap sessions, trying for sixties hipness twenty years later. Every once in a while Mary raised her hand to speak about something that was bothering her; not the loneliness, or the part-time job, or the crying that was going on inside all the time, but the fact that she had no hair, and couldn't stop cutting it. And the tough girls with tattoos, or the fat, beaten girls with no hope, themselves too scared to talk, passed her little pieces of paper saying 'hang in there', 'you can do it', 'you sound OK'.

Nobody made a pass, not that Mary was pass material, but all that shit she'd heard about dykes cruising women and coming on like truck drivers was such a load of crap. In fact, Mary thought the reverse was true. She saw that most women who are particularly sensitive to women, get real quick who is and isn't attracted to them, and would almost never come on unless guaranteed a positive response. The male posturing and bravado hid the intuition, but that didn't mean it wasn't there.

Mary was too scared to bear human touch, but sometimes she got so tired her head would fall on some big girl's street thug shoulder, and real soft the girl would say, 'It's alright, honey.' One time before Mary could talk, a jittery Spanish doll, who moments before had panicked and pulled herself together in two flashing seconds over a lost lipstick, held her for long, Latin moments. Mary was afraid of getting lost in her sensuality, her breasts and her perfume, but was also strengthened by her fierce mothering.

Mary got her part-time job by looking in the want ads. A tennis club on a roof in downtown Los Angeles hired her for five dollars an hour to stand on a busy street corner in a tennis outfit handing out advertising flyers. The Tennis Anyone Spa hoped for a girl with front office appearance, but when Mary showed up at the aging, desperate health club with earthquake cracks in the sauna, the manager gave her a little white hat to cover her head and sent her out on the street. For a few extra dollars, Toby, the boss, asked her to balance the books and teach an aerobics class to secretaries in their lunch hour.

'Who's your barber?' he asked during the initial interview.

'I am.'

'Maybe you should tip better.'

'I know.'

'It's not so bad. It'll grow back. At least you won't pick up head lice in the steamroom. Joke. Joke. You can smell the disinfectant five blocks away. I run a clean club.'

Toby was an English tennis pro with a serious eye on the American dollar. A really cheap set of hair transplants plugged into his upper forehead. They looked like bugs and Mary kept wanting to brush them off. Three rows of symmetrical dark dots of hair, a good quarter of an inch apart, was hardly state of the art surgery, but Toby thought he looked great. Every Friday Mary took him the ledgers unable to account for $1,000 here or $1,500 there. Without missing a beat, he told her to put it under 'lost tennis balls'.

'They go over the roof into the street, and we never see them again.' She quietly understood that $5,000 worth of lost tennis balls a month was not the whole story.

Toby's idea of the good life was owning three or four tract houses in Redondo Beach, a Southern California slum with palm trees. He proudly told Mary how he beat the system. He showed her his very large state property tax bills all demanding payment and finally announcing takeover of the property. 'But here's the thing, they never check. They take your house only on paper!' In the meantime Toby collected a nice rent on his confiscated houses. He seemed to have no stress factor. He sent Mary down to the tax board and told her to ask for extensions, drowning the secretaries in circuitous paper work. After literally hours in

13

line, Mary suspected that this foreigner's objective evaluation of the tax bureaucracy was very astute, if unethical.

Mary also posted tennis flyers in every ladies room in the ten or twelve skyscrapers that compose the downtown L.A. area. The bathroom job was okay, preferable in fact to the people on the street corner looking at her legs. On the twenty-second floor of the Interstate Bank Building, Mary found a ladies room with a sofa. Eureka. She could take naps. Resting was not allowed in the Begin Again Home for Women. The regimen was bearable, but the daily required homework of goal lists and life plans used up most of the energy needed for actual work. It took imagination to come up with the crap the social workers wanted to hear. The residents, who hoped mainly for their own place and a lover who wouldn't steal their money, strained over yellow pads to write thesis ideas for Ph.D.'s they were going to get while working full time and raising little Cody and Jennifer. The woman who taught the 'Live Your Dreams' seminar expected nothing less. The angrier girls pointed to their crotches and said 'Dream this', but Mary tried to work the system and exhausted herself in the process. Sleeping on the job was the only break. Mary also took naps in the Bonaventure Hotel. The cleaning ladies didn't seem to mind if she put two chairs together in the powder room.

One night Toby invited Mary and the rest of the staff to his personal house for an employee dinner. 'We'll have steak,' he said, like he was serving gold. The outside of the house was brown, as was the inside panelling and rug. The curtains were Howard Johnson orange and the kitchen cabinets inexplicably opened with huge brass Byzantine handles. Toby set up his grill on the cement space he called the yard, and for the next three hours the guests rotated their plastic beach chairs around the barbecue avoiding smoke as the wind changed.

'Ramon, I've heard there's a new caulking that stands up under sauna heat. We should plug that crack near the bottom bench. Some kind of fungus is growing up the wall.' Toby talked shop as he flipped T-bones on the six dollar bargain hibachi. The coals weren't hot, and he kept squirting lighter fluid around the steaks.

'It sears the meat. It'll be delicious. Mary, help me out here. You haven't got any hair to singe. I've got $5,000 worth of implants going up in flames.'

Mary held the fork as far from her body as possible and stabbed at the meat. Ramon drank his beer and dealt with the caulking issue.

'I know, boss, I saw it at the hardware store. It's expensive.'

'No problem. Offer him tennis lessons for a few tubes.'

'He hates tennis. He wants the money.'

'We'll send Mary over there for a private aerobics class. A tutorial. Relax, Mary, I can't send him a girl who has to wear a hat day and night.'

'Maybe he's into a hat thing, boss.' Ramon laughed and rubbed his head suggestively. Mary thought she was in hell.

Her confidence boosted from safe busy nights in the halfway house, she upgraded herself by getting a part-time job in a children's store in a very good neighbourhood. Except for a patch of exposed scalp near her neck where she cut off a curl too fast, two months' growth of spotty, brown hair gave her the borderline respectability of an outpatient. It was the Saturday before Easter, so there was a frenzy of mothers fitting their children in bonnets and gloves and tiny suits. All the packages had to be wrapped with a little sprig of flowers as a holiday touch. That was Mary's job. This career move paid seven dollars an hour. Mary wore a turtleneck covered with tiny seals balancing balls on their noses, and black pants. She looked like Popo the Clown.

A pest named Lawrence came into the store to buy a sleeper for his nephew. He wanted 'Guess For Kids' and bothered Mary until she special ordered it for him. He also wanted her phone number. He wouldn't take no for an answer, and because male commotion wasn't desirable in the little mothers' shop, Mary gave it to him to shut him up.

Mary didn't want to date anyone. She wanted to work, go home to her new little apartment, eat dinner, watch TV and sleep. She was in a low cycle, as Madame Rosinka, the palm reader on Hollywood Boulevard told her. Madame Rosinka gasped when she looked at Mary's left hand and shook her head. 'Unclear, unclear' she repeated as Mary forked up twenty dollars. Big news, thought Mary, as she turned down Madame Rosinka's forty dollar offer of spiritual help. The fortune teller wasn't a total fake, however, as she puzzled over the hand. 'I see a woman, but I don't understand. Come back in two weeks. I read again.'

There was a moment when Mary first met Heather when she stopped hearing their words and saw only the thousands of hairs on Heather's face. It was as if some chemical had been released behind her eyes that did for her perception what adrenaline does for the body. She saw keenly and with great detail. There was no judgement. In this instant, Heather was not a man or a woman, pretty or ugly; she was just there. And in her act of observation, Mary was there too. It was a moment of pure loving. Mary didn't know this at the time. To her, love was a later evaluation of preciousness, beyond this first clear moment of acceptance.

Heather had honked and picked Mary up as she was walking in a barren stretch of Hollywood. Mary was walking because her car had broken down.

They knew each other from around. Mary had seen her at the Hollywood Bowl, carrying her own cushions for the hard wooden benches that were the cheap seats. She looked like a madwoman on this occasion with a circle of separateness around her. She didn't engage with the environment.

For a time, the craziness threw Mary off the track of her beauty. At the summer concert, Heather found her section, row, and seat number like a bag lady. She used too much concentration for the task, and even the ushers stayed away, but when she smiled and stood with the crowd for an encore ovation she was a tall, graceful woman with long hair that seemed to reflect her dual temperament. There is a wild kind of hair that is suitable for sexy shampoo ads and sultry ladies. With Heather this same enviable prop sometimes went awry and suggested Medusa. When it didn't go awry, she was a knockout with supernatural blue eyes. She had tiny teeth. Raymond Chandler made an enormous impression on Mary as a young reader when he described one of his neurotic and finally evil women as having tiny teeth. This swift negative association also kept Mary from seeing her beauty until they were well into it.

Heather looked like a possible friend. She stared evenly at Mary with wide eyes and laughed at her jokes. When Mary cried over her broken car, Heather wrote 'accept what is' on a little shred of paper, and it fixed her like a drug. Romantic advice just promises love, but spiritual advice promises salvation. Stone blind to her motives, Mary asked Heather to have dinner with her. She had no idea she was bringing coals to Newcastle.

Dinner with Heather was peaceful. Mary talked like a magpie, reaching into her considerable bag of tricks to make Heather laugh. She started with her 'Cher' riff. Mary loved Cher, but also knew educated people considered it beneath them to love Cher, so there was a good deal of self-mockery in her routine. She talked about Cher with the excess of a true fan, and hoped her comical passion would delight the sombre Heather.

'When my ex-boss insisted I teach an aerobics class, I only played six songs. Ballads. No strain. My class was like Cher's Las Vegas act. Have you ever seen it?'

Heather shook her head.

'It's not an energetic act. Cher doesn't do anything. She stands there in the middle of the stage while six dancers, three singers, and fifty dressers whirl around her body changing her clothes every five minutes. Then she looks bored out of her mind in that drop dead way that makes you think she's just killing time before she goes back to bed. The most strenuous thing she does is change her wigs. I'm getting goosebumps all over again. It's such a relief to see a woman do nothing. I live through her inactivity. Talk about liking yourself. She shows up. Period.

'Every once in a while she walks across the stage. That's her act. Walking. But it's worth thirty-five dollars. It's the most talented walk I've ever seen. Her hips lead with a sexual confidence that gives everyone in the audience a hot little twinge. Then she gets preoccupied in a show business kind of way to let you know she's really looking for love and sex isn't everything, so she sits down and shakes her hair trying to avoid the really serious mood that's overtaking her. But too late, she sings a slow song and projects slides of her kids on the back wall, while you think of Sonny and Greg Allman and how she's made every man she's ever been with look great. Then she takes off her clothes until she's down to a few feathers, and that's it. She's cruising while the rest of us are killing ourselves.'

Mary paused as if Cher had discovered a new species. She didn't check with Heather for confirmation. Part of Mary's act was to be hopelessly impressed yet aware of her silliness at the same time. She knew it made her look very attractive. The haircut was a handicap, so she worked overtime to compensate. Mary sensed Heather liked hearing about her infatuation with the female star. It was innocent enough, but in different company, Mary might have raved about Charles Bronson.

'Then she says "Thank you, ladies and gentlemen" like Elvis. Real low and humble, but devastating, because she's going away and you're going to be lonely again. Until she does a movie or something on TV. And you live in Los Angeles, because somewhere she's out there keeping you company. Even if you work in a filthy health club for no money, because you can't stop cutting your hair, because you can't stand being a woman anymore.'

Mary faltered. Maybe it wasn't funny, how much she needed Cher's exaggerated posing to remind her there might be glamour and satisfaction in being her own sex. Mary thought she might lose Heather in the flat out, autograph-seeking loneliness behind the jokes.

She didn't flinch. Talking to Heather was like jumping into a still pond. She absorbed the chatter quietly but her seriousness did twinkle a bit when Mary's foolishness peaked. Mary loved making serious women laugh, but what she gained with a laugh, she feared she lost in respect. Serious women could never quite accept that a clown who loved Cher and nighttime network TV could write poetry as well.

Mary kept poems in her kitchen table drawer. Disciplined and artful, reflecting intense hours with a thesaurus and her head, she didn't show them to anybody. Mary thought everybody laughed at poetry, and she herself didn't have the attention span to read it very often. She was always speeding along too fast to stay with an image, but when enough exhaustion and reality pulled her back on standard time, Mary sat still and put her fantasies on paper. She wrote during transitional periods; on aeroplanes or when somebody left town. It gave her a sense of her own presence during partings. She escaped conscious feeling as she drove her transient friends to various airports. Then she constructed a poetical system of telepathy through dreams.

Raymond, her friend and neighbour, was the only one allowed to read the poems. He liked Mary and told her to stop writing, they were too sad. He said it by the mandatory swimming pool outside his apartment. Most buildings in East Hollywood had one, but there were no playgirls lying around getting a tan in animal print bikinis. Instead planeloads of immigrating Armenians, dressed in clothes for the Baltics, sat by their little twenty by ten foot pools playing cards and making car payments on Oldsmobiles and Chevrolets no native Californian would own, petrol prices being what they were.

The glamorous automobiles were symbols of the good life portrayed in the same influential movies that featured the party girls living somewhere in the city that kept its best parts secret.

One poem, called *Dear Buddy*, was about their friendship. It touched him, but he was troubled by Mary's other poems, filled with longing and isolation. His littlest voice asked her to stop writing. She heard the concern in his tone and knew it was not literary criticism, but a friend's compassion, and it stuck with her for months.

Heather asked Mary up to her apartment after they had dinner. There is a touch of fantasy in even the plainest Hollywood apartment. A slum is painted hot pink, a cracker box has a pond with live carp, a man's home is literally a castle. Heather's apartment had a waterfall running down the side of the building.

Mary, not one to relax easily, felt immediately comfortable in Heather's apartment. Heather momentarily lost her sang-froid when she saw her bills laid out on the floor. 'Can you budget?' she asked Mary. Mary managed small amounts of money well. How she managed to stay out of debt on seven dollars an hour mystified her friends, but she learned all the Depression tricks from her mother. Mixing water with the last drop of shampoo for an extra wash, using real rags from old clothes instead of paper towels, rolling pennies and cashing them in. The poverty tricks she tried so carefully to hide, became fashionable when recycling hit the middle class.

After Mary gave Heather a few economy tips, they moved from the work table to a futon, and finally settled on the floor. Heather's silence was a vacuum for Mary's chatter. She trusted Heather right away, and it was such a relief to have someone to talk to. Except for the last year in California, Mary always had a best girlfriend. This felt like that. Like sitting on a swing for hours after school talking about nothing.

Heather listened and laughed and her eyes sparkled and when Mary finally got up to go home around two a.m., Heather walked her to the door and kissed her on the mouth.

It was a fast, deliberate move, and Mary's heart turned over. Heather said she'd call at ten the next night.

· *Two* ·

On that second night, Heather called at 10.20. Mary started waiting for the call at 10.00. Between 10.00 and 10.20, Mary went from anticipation to disappointment to rage too quickly and the intensity of her emotions controlled her ability to think. It unsettled her that there was no apparent reason for the intimacy of these stronger feelings.

One New Year's Eve, new friends had invited Mary to a floating underground club that was having a party. 'It will be fun, we'll meet you there.' Mary dressed up according to the fashion; a black and pink mini dress from newly emerging Melrose Avenue and took some angel dust to make a good night great. She drove to the secret basement off Sunset Boulevard by herself and waited for her new friends. The music was loud and not good. The company was too stoned and too disparate. The cool Hollywood rats and a bunch of rednecks off the bus couldn't mesh. How they'd come together in one room was anybody's guess. Mary suspected it was the promise of drugs and a good time that went out on too many networks. Well after midnight, Mary realised her friends weren't coming. She was stoned enough that her disappointment and anger burned low and passive. Mary found a large Southern boy stinking of beer and the Greyhound bus and pulled him onto a vinyl sofa. His mouth was wet and they necked and rubbed each other until he came in his pants. Mary was so far inside herself, that nothing really touched her, not his hands or his breath. She worried a little that he'd get beer on her dress. Then she went home.

The second the phone rang, she forgot her distressing memory, and together Mary and Heather said 'Let's take a walk.'

They both lived on the edge of a neighbourhoood called Los Feliz. Griffith Park, and the Observatory from *Rebel Without a Cause* borders the north and Hollywood lies south and west. Los Feliz is filled with mansions from the old days. W.C. Fields, William Randolph Hearst and Marion Davies built homes in these hills, and Mary walked where Sal Mineo, Natalie Wood and James Dean acted out their first identified passion of friendship and loneliness. Eucalyptus trees silhouetted against the glow of the city recalled images from *Gone With The Wind* and *Psycho*. So many scenes in so many movies were shot in Los Angeles that this kind of overlapping was possible, Mary supposed. Separating myth from current reality was a constant low-level pressure for Mary in Hollywood.

Los Feliz was still romantic. The mist came off

the park and year-round Christmas lights decorating the more extreme fantasy homes confused seasonal memory and kept the neighbourhood in a permanent Disney trance. It was relatively safe at night, with a few homosexuals cruising the bushes for a quick encounter.

The broad Los Feliz boulevard divided the park from secluded residential streets, mostly scaled to normal non-fantasy life, but also hiding old treasures. Fabulous estates, built on the hills in layers, overlooked the smog-diffused grid of Los Angeles. The bougainvillea bloomed year round in huge banks the length of many football fields along the boulevard.

Heather and Mary walked down the private DeMille Drive. They stopped and looked through electronic gates at the massive houses. It was night-time, dark like the movies, and Mary slipped into *Wuthering Heights* for a moment; Lawrence Olivier and Merle Oberon peering over the wall into David Niven's gay, rich party. She wanted to touch Heather.

In present time, the soft air and quiet observation was shared and pleasant to both women. The pleasure was interrupted by pictures in Mary's head. Still slides dropped into the mental projector, rejected by a click of a button as they came up.

She put her arm around Heather's waist under a Eucalyptus tree. Reject. She kissed her lightly, just their heads turning, by the wrought iron gate on DeMille Drive. Reject. Mary's attraction was deepening toward this new friend who saw nothing unusual in the midnight walk in the city, but the sexual impulse was a mystery and not allowed. Mary censored herself for Heather more than anything else. Why confuse this nice quiet friend with immature expressions of devotion that would pass? But she did wonder if these prurient thoughts were hers alone or some symbiotic mind-reading of Heather's. It was hard to own up to taboo desire all by one's self, and Mary knew the romantic connection was sometimes uncanny in its shared knowledge.

The playwright Lillian Hellman, who addressed this issue, made sure her heroines were righteously angry when confronted with accusation of lust in their female friendships. Jane Fonda slugged the man who insinuated such a leaning toward Vanessa Redgrave in *Julia*. The friendship was too pure and noble for these thoughts even to occur. Lillian Hellman made Mary want to puke.

Every sex magazine and video on the market showed girls together. If Mary landed from Mars, she would have thought American sex consisted of two naked women touching each other with a man watching. No judgement in *Penthouse* or *Playboy*, but act on these fantasies and it's queer city. If that shy nymph comes off that airbrushed page into real life, she gets fat, grows hair on her legs, drives a truck and hates men. It's a miracle.

Mary kept walking and did not reach out to hold Heather's hand. Uncool, this sweet feeling on a summer's night in Hollywood.

★ ★ ★

Heather cut short the second night of walking when she suggested Mary come upstairs and have tea. Fine with Mary, she was getting tired. Stretching out on the living room floor to talk, Mary suppressed the slightly more pornographic pictures that kept breaking her train of thought. Stir the water, squeeze the lemon, tap the Sweet 'n' Low into the cup; Mary didn't linger on the blue channel. Outside the scenes were innocent and romantic, inside they were harder. Mary couldn't walk off her energy in the apartment.

She breathed the air between Heather's hair and neck, brushing her lips against that soft place. Don't even think about it. She rested her hand on Heather's breast in the middle of a conversation on popular music. Stop. No resistance from Heather, only laughter in the eyes. Really stop.

'This tea is great. I can't drink coffee anymore. It hypes me up.' Mary regained her control.

'I know, I'm the same way.' Heather answered lying down on the floor. Mary pulled her knees up to make room. Heather was close.

Heather brushed her hair against Mary's leg. Mary ignored this, along with her fantasies. Heather did it again, lingering, almost resting her head on Mary's knee. Her eyes were warm and open, and finally she asked Mary, 'Do you want to spend the night?' It was not snowing or raining, Mary's car had not been impounded, and she lived only a few blocks away. There was no mistaking this invitation. She said yes.

Heather resembled one of the most beautiful

modern male archetypes; the early hippie, that first wave of young men with long hair who endured the kissing noises and mockery, but still smiled like Jesus, their eyes soft from pot and a real conviction that peace was better than war. They were the first males to say such a thing, and Mary remembered feeling so safe with them as they explained their radical philosophy and made love with pure, stoned wonder and innocence. The modern MTV kinkiness that's needed to juice up desire in the contagious and dangerous nineties was still asleep and confined to porno shops and whorehouses.

Heather's unglamorous hair fell around her shoulders like hippie hair, untrained by a blow dryer or a disciplined Beverly Hills cut, and she walked with the same confidence that comes only from surviving ridicule. Later, Heather would speak quietly of gang rape and the last big laugh of public lesbianism.

At fourteen, Mary had watched the half-naked, bell-bottomed men with a dizzy crush. They challenged her conservative, modest thighs with gentle voices and tambourines. With Heather, Mary wasn't just attracted to a woman, she was attracted to a woman who reminded her of her dream man. For a girl with simple tastes, Mary was about to complicate the whole show.

Heather went to the bathroom and Mary took off her clothes and got into bed. She listened to the waterfall trickling down the side of the building. The only light was street light from outside the window. In one fast, definite move, Heather entered the room, pulled her shirt over her head, and came to bed naked. Their coming together was filled with need, and release of that need. They could breathe and sigh and exhale. Their moves were fast and urgent, with very little notice of each other, except for that absorbing desire for friction. They hugged and rubbed and kissed ferociously, not like the languid magazine women with pearls in their mouths. They were too hungry to be pretty, and later, they fell asleep without talk.

In the morning, Heather dashed out of bed, and came back smelling of soap and peppermint. This was a switch. Mary always brushed her teeth for her bed partners. Role reversal is so illuminating. Mary saw her own thoughtfulness, her own desire to please and her own insecurity mirrored back at her in this simple gesture. This was going to be interesting, Mary thought, as she ran back to her apartment to change her clothes for work. She checked her machine. Lawrence, the pest, called as usual. He always called, she never called back. The morning after sex hustle from apartment to apartment was the same; the late showing up for work at the baby store in sexual disarray.

'What a big boy. He's definitely toddler size. Only eight months. How about a little football sleeper?'

'You want a party dress in black? She's only six. You're absolutely right, it won't show the dirt. I'll check in the back.'

It slowed down in the afternoon, and Mary steamed the wrinkles out of twenty-four Christening dresses, priced twelve copies of *Bible Stories for*

Children, and copied out a recipe for apple turnovers. By night a sexual deviant, by day a Presbyterian. Mary was laughing inside.

The left side of Mary's face started to ache by the second week of the affair. She held her own for about three days. Heather's words fell on her strangely as they should. When Heather asked if talking about her ex-husband made Mary jealous, Mary wanted to say gently, 'I don't even know you.' She didn't, but the thought was there. On the second morning, Heather made a breakfast of omelettes with avocado and cheese, and hashbrowns and toast with homemade jam. Mary flashed back to 1972 and the macrobiotic offerings so freely shared by long-haired boys and girls smelling of incense in the morning. This nostalgia was broken when Heather served her a plate and said, 'You must be doing something right.' Mary was both pleased, sensing perhaps a sexual compliment, and confused by the touch of trade-off in this remark. She wasn't hooked yet, so she ate a small breakfast. Domestic dyke. Culinary queer. Homosexual homemaker. A little quiet name-calling gave Mary some distance. Mary had about a week before she was absorbed completely.

They were in the shower when Heather pointed out that they were alike. 'Our skin is the same, and our bodies are the same.' This wasn't about gender; Heather seemed to think their body type was similar. Mary didn't see it. Heather was tall and big-boned. Mary was smaller by some inches in every part. Mary was kinetic and out of control most of the time, but well co-ordinated. Her grace was in speed and the avoidance of calamity as she cut through space too fast to see. Heather thought ahead. Her composure was fabulous. She was slow and deliberate, placing her hands on the coffee cup or steering wheel with apparent awareness of cause and effect.

But, because Heather was very beautiful, Mary allowed that, yes, they were alike.

'You make this so easy,' Heather said as Mary laughed and flirted with her own reflection in the mirror on Heather's bedroom door. The night Mary made it so easy was a night of love. She had learned to dress warmly in many layers like Heather. It was fall in L.A. which really happens. It gets chilly and the little gas heaters in the apartments pretending it's year-round summer, don't reach into the bedrooms and bathrooms as the temperature drops fifteen degrees in an hour, when the sun goes down. They couldn't get to their skin fast enough, as they pulled one sweater after another over their heads.

'Have you ever noticed that women take sweaters off pulling from the waist, and men take off clothes reaching behind their shoulders?' They both pulled one layer off from behind, and perceived this simple move to be so instantly boyish and different from their natural way.

Their lovemaking had not yet slowed down to any reasonable pace. Mary was orgasmic just thinking about Heather. Literally. Contractions came and went as they pleased. Now that she'd made love to a woman, she wondered seriously why men weren't aroused all the time in the presence of women, and she identified with the energy of the teenage boy. Mary often jogged the mile or so to Heather's house just to reduce her excitement to a cooler level. The unthinkable act of rape was still unthinkable, but serious coercion, involving capture, imprisonment and benevolent domination, seemed within reason.

Mary had in fact been pursued ardently by men, so what she knew about women and lovemaking she learned from men. So, what did she know? Mary was in the dark, and apart from her singular passion for Heather, she wanted to see what a woman was like.

Most of Mary's information came from Andy and Dick, her primary boyfriends. Andy came too quickly, barely out of his pants. He lived in fear that he would stain his clothes, the sheets, or the sofa. Nobody was worried Mary would get pregnant. If Andy managed to get himself halfway into Mary, that was it, it was over. He always held a towel in one hand to catch the load as he called it. Wherever it went, it rarely made it to Mary.

Andy installed a washer/dryer next to the bedroom. The moment sex was over, in went the towel, the sheets, his socks and underwear. His compulsivity was awesome. Every possession had to be new and very clean. He broke up with Mary once because she'd been the one to suggest he park in the parking lot where his BMW got a microscopic door nick.

How did Andy make up for his excitability? He talked sexy. His quickness, which he accepted with grace, 'It's you, it's you. You get me so excited,' inspired him to provide Mary with any sexual apparatus he could find worldwide. He collected vibrators. From Australia, the basic vibrator had a little rubber appendage in the shape of a kangaroo that jumped in place while the dildo itself did its work; a sort of undulating, down under motion. Texture was the big variable. State of the art plastic was not made only for aeronautics. A clear synthetic warmed instantly to the touch, retaining its basic form in action but covered with a malleable skin not unlike the original. There was a black one, a glow-in-the-dark one, fun for Halloween, an exact penis replica, and one with a satisfied woman's face carved on the tip, among others.

Mary took a look at the latest acquisition, but she could have cared less. She felt compelled to try the kangaroo the one time, but she always picked the basic slow-medium-fast ball massager with the handle.

She turned herself on slow, and Andy muted the TV, never taking his eyes off the horse races he got on cable. And he talked.

'Let go, baby, it's alright, it's OK, good girl, go, that's right, that's good. Oh, yes, baby, yes, that's nice, very nice, oh, I'm getting so excited. God, you turn me on. What am I gonna do, oh, that's right, that's good, let go, baby, that's it, oh, that feels good, yes, yes, yes.'

And he talked for as long as it took. Sometimes the rhythm accelerated as some horse he liked broke for the finish line. 'Go, go, go, go!' Mary's legs would ache with tension as she tried to keep up.

Dick her other boyfriend, couldn't come. He held onto stuff. He stayed hard for about four days. Up, down, up, down, up, down. No orgasm. Finally, she'd put his desperate penis between her breasts, and he'd moan and come all over her neck.

Also a great compensator, he beguiled with fantasy. His verbal freedom was wild and generous as his body wanted to be, but couldn't. His feminine awareness was very high for a heterosexual.

Mary's textures were schoolgirl rough; course white sheets, cotton underpants, terry cloth, and flannel.

Dick showed her there was something else. He bought her a black satin teddy with white lace on the bodice. He talked about the feel of her breast under the fabric, making a definite erotic point, but she was cold in spaghetti straps. And the satin generated electricity, so her hair got funny, and she felt little shocks and saw flashes of light under the covers.

When Mary wasn't distracted by the natural phenomena occurring in the bed, she listened to Dick talk her through her orgasm, and four days later, his.

He would have liked her to praise his size and say things like 'I want you so bad. You've got the biggest one I've ever seen, oh my God, baby, give it to me. I can't wait.' But Mary couldn't say these things.

Dick did not mind. When she hesitated, he talked for her. 'You want me so bad. Look at this. This is the biggest one you've ever seen. Oh, God, baby, you want it so bad. I'm the best. Oh God, you can't wait.'

After talking, pumping, praising, and teasing, he finally finished, and gasped, 'You're great. My God, Mary.'

Years later, he would knock on her door once in a while, somehow sensing the moments when she was alone and vulnerable, and through the screen door, whisper, 'Don't say a word. Don't do anything.'

Following her into the kitchen, he'd pin her up against the refrigerator, and dress her in an imaginary outfit, 'You're wearing high heels and nothing else. I'm taking off my tie and putting it around your naked neck between your breasts. I'm undoing my belt. Put it around your waist.' Mary hinted once that she liked to be naked with a man in a three-piece suit. Dick owned one suit and vest and wore it every time for years. In point of fact, he usually caught Mary in her terry cloth robe with her hair in hot oil, and face red and blotchy from waxing her upper lip and plucking her eyebrows.

He didn't see her that way. She was a siren always, and for this alone, Mary would open her robe and hold him as he frantically tried to let go of all the lessons that taught him to keep it in and be quiet.

Dick and Andy were the boys Mary brought to bed with Heather. Not literally, but they were there. She also brought a gesture of love from her mother. Mary's mom always changed the sheets when little Mary got sick in the middle of the night. It was a wonder to Mary, that while she threw up the occasional flu bug or bad meat, her mother made up a fresh bed. Mary thought this was the nicest thing that anybody had ever done for her. Whenever Heather got a cold, Mary changed the sheets. It was an expression of feeling lost on Heather. But who could expect her to read a mind that thought clean sheets was a love poem.

'I'm not having any orgasms.'

'You're not?' Mary said, somewhat confused.

'No, I'm not.'

'Oh, I'm sorry, I didn't realise.' Didn't realise, you could have knocked her over with a feather. Mary's passion was so intense, she couldn't grasp that perhaps Heather was having a different experience. Her blindness was in devotion, not in thoughtlessness, and for one second a little chink of light opened allowing some shared sympathetic feeling with maleness and its apparent insensibility. All Mary wanted in the world was to please this woman, so there was no particular ego blow in the information. Mary quite practically just had to find another way. Andy and Dick helped her.

She didn't miss a beat. She got close to Heather's ear, and very softly told her a story. It was a corny story, using a number of corny sex images from *Penthouse* including a Victorian wing back chair and a male voyeur.

Mary, confused about her response to pornography, had read an erudite article in the *New York Times*, which explained to her that if she got aroused by looking at naked women in *Playboy* or *Penthouse*, it was because she identified with the girls. She became the girl in the picture.

Heather thought little of the *New York Times* analysis, and made Mary laugh when, leafing through *Penthouse*, said, 'I don't want to be the girls, I want to be *with* the girls.'

'I want to be with the girls in *Vogue* and *Harpers Bazaar*,' said Mary. 'Do you remember Jean Shrimpton, oh my God? And so beautifully dressed.'

They laughed, pulling out of the pictures and into each other, together for the time being.

Mary's corny story worked. Heather had her orgasm and Mary was quite satisfied with herself, as Heather jumped out of bed to go to work at her typewriter in the other room. Mary's neck hurt a little from leaning into Heather's ear, and as she stretched to ease it, she felt her own unsatisfied state of arousal. Her symbiotic pleasure with Heather's orgasm was good but she wanted more. She thought about being with a man, and tried to dismiss the female coupling as ultimately adolescent and unsatisfying, but remembered she wanted more from the boys too. She barely started attacking herself and Heather for perversity, and worse, frustrated perversity, when she felt Heather's hand on her shoulder and her softest breath on her neck whispering, 'I missed you in the other room.' Heather's long body stretched next to hers and they left the world of Victorian wing back chairs and male voyeurs and joined each other in the tenderness and compassion of each other's eyes.

When Heather asked Mary to take care of her, Mary got confused. Who will take care of me, was her instinctual first thought, which she quickly ignored in her desire to please. She started to work longer hours. She needed money to hold her own with Heather's income. Heather, the big-boned Amazon who took only one step to Mary's two, was fragile, and Mary danced around her needs with no thought of herself. Her car became her closet as she assumed the role of suitor. She got up an hour early to shower, run home to check the machine and get to work.

Heather cooked. Mary had a wife. It was then that Mary got angry in the strangest political way. It had become funny and fashionable for busy straight professional women to say they wanted a wife. Did they understand that in wanting a wife, they became the husband? Or like Heather, did they want to be the wife and have the wife. Mary was tripping all over her feminism, as she worked two jobs to be able to take Heather to the movies on a Saturday night, and God forbid Heather didn't want to have sex. Mary was turning into a male chauvinist pig.

So they discussed it. They cried, they said they'd change. Maybe more time apart. Maybe more time together.

'I'll drive.'

'No, that's OK, I'll drive.'

'No, really, I feel like driving.'

'Are you sure?'

'Absolutely.'

'This traffic is terrible. We're going to be late.'

'I told you we should have left earlier.'

'So now it's my fault.'

'No, I didn't mean it that way. I'm sorry. Idiot, moron driver can't put on his clicker?' Heather put her hand on Mary's thigh. They smiled. They made up.

'What movie do you want to see?'

'I don't care.'

'No, really, tell me the truth.'

'*Rambo: First Blood part II.*'

'Be serious.'

'I am serious.'

'I want to see *Manon of the Spring*.'

'Sub-titles.'

'So?'

'I've been reading all day.'

'Well, I can't do *Rambo*.'

They stayed at home and watched TV.

'Are you sleeping with Patty?'

'No.'

'She wants to sleep with you.'

'No, she doesn't. She likes men.'

'Bull.'

'I hate jealousy.'

'Well, I hate Patty.'

They broke up. Heather found somebody else to take care of her within a week. And Mary wondered if it was such a hot idea to date women.

But a man was out of the question, as she cried her body to sleep, desperate enough for Heather to look for a replacement. The rejection hallucinations had started. Glimpses of Heather in candlelight restaurants and orchestra seats bothered Mary like LSD tracers interrupted vision months after ingestion. How Heather managed to get invited to the Academy Awards was a mystery until Mary focused on the television and realised she was watching Jacqueline Bisset find her seat.

Lawrence dropped into the baby store to remind Mary he was still interested. He impressed her with his ability to take repeated rejection. When she said no, he still tried to make her laugh, still tried to turn her no into a maybe, and still dropped his change when she looked him in the eye. He was short in size but told her right off he was quick and smart. He was pursuing Mary.

She liked his style and thought it might work with Joanne. Mary was pursuing Joanne.

Joanne was a dyke. Her name should have been Turk. Mary figured her measurements were 46-46-46, with the top figure counted mostly across her back. Joanne carried her body with the low centre of gravity of a natural biker. Mary didn't hesitate to get on a motorcycle with her. It was safe. With the sensitivity of a tabloid newspaper reporter, Mary saw only a cliché. One size fits all. Maybe a tough gender-bender would take care of her for a change. Joanne's drawing card was her soft, brown eyes with so much hurt in them, Mary knew it was for life. Joanne's adoption out of a foster home came late in childhood, and she saw her unpopularity as permanent.

'Popular girls have always liked me though,' she told Mary. Mary was popular in the halfway house circle. Girls were always yelling 'Hey, Mary' out of their pickups on the freeway.

Mary asked Joanne out for coffee three times before she accepted. Coyness came as a surprise. Mary expected a click of the heels or a clap on the back, but got instead a tilted head and a flirtatious 'maybe another time'. Finally Joanne agreed, and said Mary could pick her up at 7.30. Mary washed and filled the car, and spied the waiting Joanne pacing on a small balcony halfway down the block. At a distance she resembled Heathcliff; dark, brooding and relentlessly masculine. They went to a House of Pies on the corner of Sunset and Silver Lake, where nobody questioned anybody's sex too seriously. It was a relief for Mary to sit with this woman who'd given up even the slightest pretence of appearing pretty. She needed a shave, which Mary would have needed if she didn't drip hot wax on her upper lip and rip out the hairs twice a month.

'So, I guess I'm gay,' Joanne said in a monotone. There was no music in her voice. All her sentences had the same flat delivery, no emotion allowed.

'I sort of didn't do anything until I met this girl Heather.' Joanne continued, 'She wanted me to take care of her and I really loved her, but she dumped me. I think she wanted somebody richer.'

Mary's stomach dropped the way it does when a 747 jetliner hits turbulence. Her Heather let this Cro-Magnon touch her.

'Could we have the check please?' Mary hailed the ancient waitress who looked like she came to town thinking she was another Lucille Ball. Joanne grabbed the check, flipped her wallet out of her back pocket, paid the cashier, and stuck a toothpick in her mouth. 'That's okay. I worked this week. I've got money.'

'When you've got two sexes to work with, you think it would be easy to get a date.' Mary told her neighbour, Raymond, who understood. 'But it's not. The guys want to fuck you right away and the girls want to talk about it forever. Except for Heather, of course, who sleeps with everyone.' Watching Heather change partners was not a major theme over the next two years, but still and all it was a nuisance.

They sat on a little terrace off the kitchen listening to the wind chimes.

'I want to marry every guy I meet,' said Raymond. 'But everybody's got someone else they're really in love with that I remind them of. If I had a dollar for every guy I remind somebody of, I'd be rich and wouldn't have to go through this bullshit.'

'You know, you do remind me of Heather a little bit.'

'I'm a chameleon, a generic man-woman, a clone.'

'Stop, you're one of a kind. I don't know what I'd do if I didn't know you. So what do you think, should I take Joanne out again? You know, just overlook this coincidence?

'Well, if there's some movie you're just dying to see and you don't want to go alone, and I'm busy, then maybe.'

Mary hesitated for a couple of weeks until the phone rang all by itself. Joanne said there was a French film playing in an art house out by the beach that she really wanted to see. She'd drive. That was all Mary needed. If somebody offered to drive, she'd say yes to anything.

This film was so obscure, Mary couldn't find any reviews. It was about a French bag lady, who rode around in French boxcars looking chic, and then died in a ditch from the cold. Joanne loved it. Mary had a little trouble staying awake, but was willing to discuss the theme of hopelessness, as long as they could go eat somewhere.

Mary woke up when she saw a pet store next to the theatre. She wanted to get a closer look at the three parrots sitting on a tree in the middle of the shop. Not fifteen feet into Casa de Pets, Joanne grabbed Mary rigid and shaking. Mary didn't get it at first, thinking this was a somewhat abrupt intimacy. She looked at Joanne's face and saw instead real terror. In her low beaten voice, Joanne moaned 'snake, snake'. Mary steadied her, then saw the caged python.

'Get me out.' Joanne begged, almost crying with fear.

'It's OK. Come on, it's in a cage. Let's go.' Mary protected her and practically carried her to the door.

Outside, the hulking Joanne was fragile and quiet. 'I guess I must really be a lesbian, I just can't stand them.'

'Well, nobody likes snakes that much,' comforted Mary, unconsciously supporting the idea that a lesbian was a bad thing to be. She wondered at Joanne's extreme phobic reaction and what it meant.

'Let's go get some Thai food. It's on me.'

'What do you think, you can buy me?' growled Joanne, turning really tough after the snake incident. Well, it had occurred to Mary, but she also wanted to be nice and treat her terrified date to something special.

The evening was a dud, but even so, Mary felt less lonely after Joanne dropped her off. They talked about petrol prices on the way home, and whether hi-test was better for the engine. She was either less lonely or relieved to be alone. Joanne had clarified something for her over dinner. She told Mary that when she walked into a crowded room all she saw were the women. 'I don't even see the men. It's like they don't exist.' Mary identified and realised how blind she'd gone.

· *Three* ·

'What could it hurt? I'll buy you dinner. You'll give me a blow-job. Just kidding, kidding. Come on, a little dinner. I just want to talk.' Lawrence talked fast under the Winnie The Pooh mobiles in the baby store.

'I've told you no a million times. I don't like men,' said Mary, laughing in spite of herself at his insistence.

'That's OK. I don't like them that much either. We have a lot in common. I know a Chinese place in Westwood. We'll eat and go see *Rocky V*. I've been wanting to see that picture.'

'Are you serious, you're the only one I know who wants to see it. I've been dying to see it but no one will go with me.'

'Fine, it's settled. Food and Sylvester Stallone. We won't have that bad of a time.'

Mary went back to steaming the twenty-four sailor suits that made up the toddler boy's spring line. She supposed she could endure one evening with Lawrence, while she was still plugging away with Joanne.

Nothing was too good for Joanne as Mary tried to pursue her in the traditional patient manner. Raymond, who worked in audience development, gave them house seats to *Phantom*, and they approached something close to intimacy when they both responded favourably to the percussive repetition of a Philip Glass concert. Mary dressed up cute in black tights and long droopy sweaters. Joanne changed nothing as she stuck to her painter's pants and western shirt. For the matinee of *Phantom* she added silver tips and chains to her cowboy boots.

Mary filled the car and picked up Joanne for the show. She wondered if there was the slightest sexual message when Joanne opened her apartment door while fastening the silver and pearl buttons on her Roy Rogers shirt. It was a minor state of undress, but looked calculated, like she was imitating something she'd seen in the movies. Whether she was pretending to be Robert Redford or Barbra Streisand was anybody's guess.

On the drive downtown, Mary told Joanne about Heather. There is a stretch of freeway from Alvarado to Chinatown where the traffic just sits, and Mary knew Joanne was captive.

'When did you start seeing her?' Joanne asked.

'Sometime around Easter.'

'That's when we broke up.'

'Heather doesn't have a long grieving period, if you'll notice. She moved in with somebody else

47

days after we broke up. I was devastated. I thought it was true love.'

'Me too.' They both wanted to talk about Heather so badly.

Joanne started. 'Boy, did we get taken, huh?'

'I worked two jobs to afford her.'

'She lives with that Patty.'

'No, they broke up. She's with a new one now.'

'Who?'

'Some sculptress in the Valley.'

'She was popular, you know. That's something I've always wanted to be. People were drawn to her.' Joanne's normally dull eyes sparkled with memory, and Mary almost got sick to her stomach. She still needed hatred to cover her longing and disappointment.

'Jesus, Joanne, she used us. I waited on her hand and foot, and I bet you did too, and that Patty, and now Veronique or Athena or some stupid name. Next week it will be somebody else.' Joanne seemed relieved that Mary was ripping Heather apart.

'I know, but nobody that pretty ever made a pass at me before. I was dazzled.'

'Joanne, you talk like a troll. I'm attracted to you. Well, I was, before this Heather thing.'

'It's because I weigh as much as a guy. You girls, Heather and you, you feel safe with me or something.'

'I pick you up, I'm driving, I'm parking, I got the tickets. It seems to me I'm the perfect man, not you.'

'This is old-fashioned crap, Mary. This male-female role thing.'

48

'I know, but the majority of the lesbian world is still acting out the most primitive role models. Straight men and women aren't nearly as rigid. Dykes are the most unliberated women on the face of the earth.'

'Except for Heather.'

'Yes, except for Heather.'

They sat quietly in the traffic. Politics seemed to diffuse some of the anger and love they shared for Heather. Fifty dollar seats to *Phantom* distracted Mary and Joanne from their thoughts. They relaxed together in the delicious fantasy, and Mary realised that news of their common lover wasn't going to blow them apart.

Joanne was a true outcast, a pariah. Even among her marginal friends, she was the most alienated, looking for clues to the simplest actions. The torment showed on her face as she asked for a cup of coffee, or tried to find the ladies room in a restaurant without being noticed. Like Quasimodo, she hid in bell towers, or their modern equivalent, a rumour of a person, even to herself. Mary rested with Joanne. There was no banter to keep up with, no jokes to laugh at, no insights to share, no expectations to fulfil. It felt good.

'You wanna come up?' There was no inflection in Joanne's invitation to see her place. Mary parked on De Longpre on a block lined with huts. If it was sunny, Mary might have upgraded the huts to shacks. But it was raining, and Mary knew every roof on the block was leaking. It was the most expensive poverty in the country, as realtors

49

advertised 'Hollywood Bungalows' for thousands of dollars a square foot. New Americans from Armenia and Iran slowly moved in next to the actors and writers and set decorators, who painted the rotting plaster and wood with an energy fired by months of unemployment.

As they walked up an exposed flight of stairs on the alley side of the building, Mary heard the ting, ting, ting of the water as it hit the pots and pans Joanne had laid out on the kitchen floor.

'The bedroom's OK,' Joanne told Mary, making it clear she was talking about dryness, not a sexual invitation, as she continued. 'Don't get any ideas, I just meant we might have to sit in there because it's not leaking.'

'This is the living room.' On the one wall not covered with shuttered windows closed against the rain, but still exposing inches of the outside where the warped angles couldn't meet, was a painting.

'Oh, yeah, I forgot to tell you, I'm a painter. Well, you know, I paint. My money comes from graphics for the movies. They put me in a room way in the back where nobody has to look at me, and I do their logos and shit.' She handed Mary a perfect rendering of the Tristar Pegasus.

The painting hung from ceiling to floor and showed a cathedral doorway, ornate like the churches in Mexico. At the foot of the massive Gothic entrance were two swarthy, muscular women dressed in short tight skirts. One was kneeling and one was standing. It was unclear whether one woman knelt in supplication before the other woman or in supplication to the church and God.

'Is it erotic or spiritual?' asked Joanne.

'I don't know but it's turning me on.' Mary made the stupid joke to cover how moved she was by Joanne's passion. The light went out of Joanne's eyes, as Mary minimized her question.

'No, no, Joanne, it's wonderful. I'm a jerk. I wasn't expecting you to talk that way. I didn't know you were going to be serious. I've been alone too much. I don't know how to talk. It's me, it's not you. Please tell me about the painting.'

Joanne's face didn't know how to smile, but she softened a little with Mary's apology.

'Yeah, well, Mexico. I went down there with some girl I was trying to sleep with. She was pretty, you know, and I figured she wouldn't care about being seen with me if we were in Mexico. I thought if I slept with her I'd become pretty. It would rub off or some stupid thing. Well, she teased me all up, wearing a bikini and shit. But I couldn't move. I paid the bills and looked at the cathedrals while she made it with a bus boy. I guess that's why I ended up with Heather. She always made the first move.'

'She did with me too. I was dying to, but it's hard, isn't it?'

'Yeah.' said Joanne.

'I imitate the way boys do it, because that's all I know. I pay the bill, then I pounce. Or I try to talk dirty. Oh, God. I turn those guys down. Why do I think it will work on somebody else?'

51

'Yeah, well, so you like the painting, huh?'

'Yes, thank you for showing it to me. God, it's really pouring. I'd better go. My street always floods in the rain.'

'OK.' Joanne perked up, knowing she wouldn't have to contend with a pass. Mary perked up knowing she wouldn't make one.

People assumed they were a couple and they got invited to anonymous houses in prosperous working class neighbourhoods, nice but undesirable in some major way. Like Altadena, up flat against the San Gabriel mountains, with the same trees and grass and driveways as any other place, but trapping the smog from the entire Los Angeles basin, the air so brown Mary couldn't see to the end of the block. A block where Joanne's friends finally bought the fifth house, their dream with a porch and room for a den off the back.

Phyllis was building it by hand. She and her lover, Cindy, chain-smoked and argued, but stayed safe from parents, fellow workers and the malls. TV reception wasn't that great either, so they weren't bombarded by the demanding female standards of *Dallas* reruns and *Knots Landing* and matte lipstick versus gloss.

Phyllis was great, at peace with herself as she welcomed Mary with two tough hands. She was old and wore her overalls like a farmer. There was facial hair on the sides of her cheeks, which she obviously shaved, giving her the steel-coloured jaw of Richard Nixon. Mary amazed herself as she involuntarily became shy and forgetful, reacting in much the same way as she might to an attractive man. She uncrossed her modest legs, forcing herself to see the clearly female breasts below the military haircut and five o'clock shadow. Mary's sweater, worn at mini-skirt length over black tights, seemed overly decorated and busy for this occasion marked by women who dressed for practicality and function.

Cindy was nervous, and apologised to Mary for her whole life as she was introduced.

'It's a nice house, isn't it?' She begged for Mary's approval, as she showed off her new wallpaper in the foyer. Education and maybe Boston coloured her speech as she tried desperately to present a traditional suburban housewife. Phyllis steadied her with a hand on her back and committed eyes. Mary sensed she was the first guest in a long time, and raved about the wallpaper and the porch. Cindy continued to flutter.

'I've made Ambrosia Salad with a new recipe I found in one of those magazines. *Good Housekeeping* or *Family Circle*. Or was it *Woman's Day*? I don't get them, of course, but I saw it in the dentist's office, and asked if I could clip it. The receptionist was so nice, she said I could take the whole magazine. Wasn't that sweet? I chipped a tooth the other day. The dentist said my teeth are brittle. What does that mean? Does it happen with age? Not that I'm that old, for God's sake, but I just bit down and a tooth broke. I mean they fixed it right away. It wasn't serious or anything, but I'm scared to eat hard foods now, or ribs.'

'Honey, how 'bout we show them the dogs.' Phyllis interrupted.

'Oh, yes, we have dogs, three corgis, just like Queen Elizabeth. I know it's silly, but I always wanted dogs when I was little, and now we have the space. A dog in an apartment, well, it's just not fair, and Phyllis built a house for them in the back. They're our kids, you know what I mean? You have to be careful here though, the coyotes come down from the mountains and try to fight. We also get deer, with the drought, they come right into the backyard, looking for water. The dogs go crazy. I tell you. Would you like some coffee? I've got a fresh pot. Phyllis bought me a new Coffee Master. God knows I like my coffee.'

Mary never drank coffee, but took a cup. Cindy needed her to take some so badly.

The doorbell rang and Cindy ran to answer. Two more women with bowls of food covered with cling film stood on the porch. The low centre of gravity and imitated male energy marked these two as they said hello. Cindy buzzed around thanking them for the chicken wings and green salad.

'You know I was worried we wouldn't have a vegetable, but I see you've put broccoli in the salad. What a good idea, and snow peas. Where did you find them this time of year?'

'We grow them.' Sally, the new visitor, spoke up. 'Yeah, we've got a vegetable garden. I grew the lettuce. You may find some bugs, but no insecticides.'

'Well, I'm impressed.' Cindy flirted gently, the happy housewife.

Joanne, monosyllabic in the corner, sort of said she was hungry.

'It's all set up, Joanne. Just help yourself. Look, I found paper napkins with dogs on them. Aren't they adorable?'

'Yeah,' said Joanne.

The ladies ate and Cindy relaxed a bit when she saw the company wasn't going to hurt her. Sally Coster and Belinda Wooten had just come back from a camping trip on Lake Piru. Mary's first sexual judgement, pegging the girls into a slot for easy dismissal, gave way to fresh observation when Sally, a natural storyteller, took over the room. She still smelled of patchouli, as if the last twenty years hadn't happened, and her greying hippie hair framed a face that glowed from remembered love-ins and gentle braless dancing with thin young men who wore American flags on their jeans. Gradually, she'd fallen away from the boys when the violence of tear gas and a burning Buddhist monk convinced her she couldn't stop war with her tie-dyed skirts and loving eyes. She was so terrified, she sank back into the feminine, swaying her hips until Belinda found her. Buffed for the nineties, with tight jeans and Elvis hair, Belinda was a thin young girl with a peace sign on her back and a CD collection of The Beatles, The Stones, and The Doors.

'Lake Piru is out-of-sight.' Sally's quiet voice lulled the women out of their defensive postures until they breathed easy with her sweet nature.

'There's nobody there. I took off all my clothes and pretended I was an Indian. In the middle of the orange groves I walked naked, smoking a joint and looking for herbs. The river's way down because of the drought, but it's clear, and I sat in it for hours reading a book to cool off. *Grist for the Mill* by Ram Dass. I read it once a year. The water just hit my shoulders, and no one bothered me. It was perfect.

'At dusk we made a fire and kept it going all night. You could see the glow through the tent and hear the cows lowing right up close. Most of the land is pasture and big black cows wander all through the hills.'

'I love cows.' Cindy piped up.

'Yeah.' Joanne agreed.

They helped themselves to devilled eggs and coldcuts, complimenting each other on every recipe for the pot-luck buffet like ladies do. The sounds of female chatter filled the room, but something was different about this hen party, girl's night out, coffee klatch. Mary couldn't put her finger on it until later when she realised that none of the women had mentioned even in passing, men. Not an inference, not a nagging story about a handyman's undone work, not a passing nod to some man's income or sexual prowess, no son-of-a-bitch Jack, no darling Bill, no adulterous Tom.

Mary's mind wandered and her eyes drifted out of the window where she saw a guy in an undershirt mowing a neighbour's lawn. In present company it was like sighting a rare species, and Mary shaded her eyes with her hand to keep her activity hidden. A slight belly bulged over his pants. He'd suck it in for a minute, then let it out when his machine tripped over a rock or protested some turn. Mary watched his steady determination as he threw obstacles into the gutter or backed up to find a smoother route. For one private, inadmissable second, she wanted to whisper through the open window, 'I miss you.'

Instead, she ate her Ambrosia Salad, treating herself to a second helping of gluey marshmallows and mandarin orange sections. Mary held onto her sentimental, yin-yang fantasy until she remembered his attractiveness was two hundred feet away and it would surely be shattered if the dumb schlub got much closer or talked to her for any length of time.

The girls were quiet for a while. Cindy calmed down and the dogs came around to be petted, settling themselves next to stalwart Phyllis. The birds seemed to get louder, as the women's need to pretend they were anything other than what they were receded. Everyone in the group except Phyllis spent most of their daylight hours acting. They were exhausted from it, and revelled in the intermission.

· *Four* ·

It would be impossible to detail Mary's story without mentioning the neighbourhood, Hollywood, and the women who actually get paid for acting. Just because she hid in the high-rise ladies rooms and halfway houses, didn't mean her life wasn't touched by the mythology that surrounded everybody in town. Ironically, she brought some of it from home.

When they were children, Jasmine lived across the street. She wasn't called Jasmine then, she was Jeannie and they were friends. Everyday after school, they met on their bicycles pumping the muscles that finally sculpted Jasmine's into some of the best legs in the world.

Both their fathers were wild. Drinking men, who razzle-dazzled but burnt out fast, like two male ants who fertilize the whole female colony then fly higher and higher until they drop dead from exhaustion. Jasmine and Mary looked at each other and knew it was their fathers' erratic spirit that lived inside them, and they vowed separately and together to honour their fathers by being stronger.

With Jasmine the first thing you saw was pretty. Why go any further? But pretty wasn't a concept when they were eight and together they passed all the more important children's tests. If the house was haunted they looked for the ghosts. 'No Trespassing' meant 'go right in' to these girls. The word 'undertow' pulled them into the ocean on a dare, and they were momentarily humbled as they got thrown hard into the sand. Jasmine cut her lip and needed three stitches which gave her mouth an off-kilter sensuality that critics later found very special.

In their anonymous teens, they went on strict beauty regimens together, little flawless girls with mudpacks on their faces talking about sex and books. Jasmine read. In any given month she read everything on the best seller list. Occasionally she surprised Mary by recommending some quietly seditious feminist publication.

Nobody even guessed at the spirit and tenacity hidden beneath the laser-perfect looks. Jasmine's drive brought her to Hollywood also and in a remarkably short time she became a movie star. A clean cut family style heroine, but mysterious and wonderful nonetheless. As recognition for her beauty devalued every other quality, Jasmine abandoned her intellect. She didn't need it anymore, but her instincts remained keen and Mary remembered who she really was. Mary hid a good deal of the difficulty of her life from Jasmine, and Jasmine minimised the extent of her celebrity to Mary. By keeping a few things secret, they became generous friends. It was a lovely thing.

But the friendship wasn't happening in Iowa at the mall where they met for coffee while raising a couple of kids. All the qualities Mary liked in her friend, in fact the essence of the woman, was public domain. Mary had to learn to share. With millions. For this reason the balance was precarious, so separations and secrecy served them well. Not that anything could really be hidden between them. They dreamt of each other's plane arrivals and departures with uncanny accuracy; it was just that some things went unsaid. Like how Mary was learning to love men by dating women, for instance. Jasmine's secret was equally radical in its own way; she was bored to death being a movie star.

At first, Jasmine's idea of being a famous Hollywood actress was like everybody else's; formed by the movie magazines she'd read as a kid. There was the compulsory big house, the compulsory Jaguar, and the compulsory designer wardrobe, flashier and showing more skin than its New York counterpart. It was, without question, the best cliché. Mary realised that movie stars were even more influenced by movie stars than normal people. The stars were the ultimate fans, pledging their lives to emulation.

Always one for taking action, Jasmine would call Mary on a Saturday and announce, 'Today we're going to learn golf.' Done up in a fetching scarf, she'd rent the equipment for both of them and spend the afternoon imitating Katherine Hepburn.

'I feel like I'm in a 1950's copy of *Photoplay*,' Mary complained as she replaced a large divot of grass as they tore up the seventh hole.

Jasmine pinned her with a single look that said something like 'civilised people throughout the ages have played incomprehensible sporting games, and if it's good enough for them, it's good enough for you.'

Tennis went without saying, horseback riding, jet-skiing at Big Bear. Mary drew the line at hand-gliding, but watched her brave friend soar over the hills at San Juan Capistrano, perhaps in a Douglas Fairbanks Jr state of mind.

Occasionally Jasmine's husband was tired or working and Mary would get some spectacular invitation. What would have been a traditional girls' night out in Cincinnati was a movie premiere in Hollywood. Jasmine never made a negative comment about Mary's ridiculous hair. Mary suspected that identity problems were all in a day's work for the actress, but Jasmine did help her pick a suitable outfit for sashaying through paparazzi. It was nothing that special, except for the colour, turquoise blue, which was particularly photogenic.

Maybe for the combative actors like Sean Penn and Marlon Brando, the paparazzi were guerrilla snipers, but with Jasmine they were lovers. 'Jasmine, over here,' they would whisper in soft petal voices just before the light bulb flashed. She could have been posing for her mother's photo album, as she smiled calmly dead into the camera's eye.

When it came to Jasmine's sex appeal, Mary put on blinders. It was a pink elephant she chose to ignore. Mary suspected that she was sexy too in a less exhibitionistic, not for everybody kind of way. But like their fathers before them they chose to transform their erotic connection into talk and movement, and a love for demanding games that held their concentration above their almost constant sexual awareness of people and situations.

After making dozens of movies, Jasmine could do it in her sleep. The roles were dull beyond belief; luminiscent girlfriends in endless buddy pictures, triumphant victims in the better horror movies, and occasionally a sexy, complex turn in a prestigious East coast hit that got her more money and more work in more buddy pictures and horror films. Acting was so easy for Jasmine, her imagination was so fluid, that all the Sturm und Drang of research and neurotic emotional dredging didn't figure. She could cry on a dime, and her empathy was such that she identified quickly and deeply with many kinds of women. For Jasmine, being a movie star became just an incredibly well-paying job, while real life supplied her with the mystery and charge most people get out of the movies. During Mary's first year at Toddler Togs, the girls rediscovered each other. Mary had the kind of real life that rich, married women find so intriguing.

Jasmine was in town looping *Speak No Evil* when she first visited Mary at the baby store. 'Oh, how nice,' she whispered in her real voice, looking at the idealised presentation of toddler life. She and her husband Peter just had their first baby, a little boy, and wanted everything to be picture perfect. Jasmine's eyes literally twinkled when she told Mary how adorable she looked in her turtleneck covered with performing seals with balls on their noses. This was where Mary parted company with Jasmine and the other friends who surfaced from her past.

Mary had been smart. Smart enough to go to a college catering to a few smart girls and many rich ones. Heiresses. These were girls to whom, incomprehensibly, the words 'waitress' and 'salesgirl' and 'receptionist' held magic. While Mary had been dazzlingly successful in burying both her smartness and her past, sometimes an old chum from Darien, Connecticut, would trace her down, gushing with admiration for Mary's latest menial job.

'Oh, Mary, you have a real job. How nice. Once I asked my father if I could be a waitress for the summer on Martha's Vineyard, and he said absolutely not. I was devastated. I wanted to wait on tables more than anything else in the world. God, I wanted to work. You're so lucky. A salesgirl. How fascinating. Can you work a cash register? That always looked like so much fun to me. The ring of the bell and making change.'

Sarah, from Connecticut, poured her heart out. She'd married a peer, a boy she'd known since she was four. They had three gorgeous children, protected by trust funds from birth, a house that made *Architectural Digest*, and some real degree of happiness, but in a world that generally condescended to Mary's position, Sarah envied her. Mary had to laugh. If an endless string of shitty jobs gave her some mystique, who was she to argue.

· *Five* ·

Two weeks after her visit, Jasmine called the store and in an off-hand, 'I don't give a shit' manner, casually informed Mary that Elizabeth Tate was coming swimming on Sunday and would Mary like to join them. Jasmine usually interrupted Mary's life with glamorous pauses when she needed company for some escapade requiring backup.

'That would be nice,' Mary answered and Jasmine repeated that Elizabeth Tate was coming. Jasmine, usually so cool, betrayed herself with repetition. Ten years before, Liz Tate had crashed television to become a media archetype. Every year another show copied her original character hoping to cash in on stolen goods. But she retained first position. Industry know-it-alls put her down by saying it was just her looks. But the people loved her and a number of publicity-filled marriages made her a consistent tabloid favourite.

'We met at a screening of *Demon Changeling Boy*. She raved about my acting. I don't know, she seemed to mean it. She wants to be friends. Please come, she's a little overwhelming.'

'Sure, are you kidding. I didn't know people actually met her.'

'Yes, well, do you think tuna fish would be okay?'

'If it's flown in from Antarctica that day.'

'Oh God, what am I gonna serve? She seems pretty down to earth.'

'Don't worry, she probably doesn't eat.'

'You're right. She weighs about four pounds.'

'Four perfect pounds.'

Mary was a ratty guest. Her hair grew in spikey, random chopped off tufts, and she was too white to be sitting by a pool in a bathing suit with two of the prettiest women in show business.

When Liz Tate leapt up the steps cut into the hill two by two, Mary realized how flat and two dimensional TV makes everything look. Liz Tate was gorgeous. Like an endangered species, not too many of her were walking around. She radiated male and female signals simultaneously. When she talked she was a Southern flirtatious charmer with a breathy voice and tilted head, and when she moved she was an athlete, loose like a boy and fast. Cheerleader and football star in one. It was a dazzling combination.

Mary saw that Jasmine was frightened by Liz Tate. But when Elizabeth shined her incredibly bright light on Jasmine, focusing all the harnessed charm of international fame in one direction, it was impossible not to get sucked in. Mary's presence kept it light, kept them girlfriends, kept it from being what it really was. And as girlfriends, they talked about men. Mary dragged out Andy and his vibrator collection, Liz dumped on her baby-faced TV star ex, and Jasmine said she missed her husband. There was so much female in the air, they bragged about their men, reminding themselves of the primary connection. Indeed, husbands and suitors checked in on the phone throughout the afternoon.

'My calls are being forwarded here. I hope you don't mind.' Liz apologised as the phone kept ringing. All the calls were taken, as the men got the intimate voices and promises of love, but Mary saw the eyes and the eyes said they were showing off, magnets for each other on this spring afternoon. Elizabeth Tate had broken and set standards for femininity on TV playing one of the first women detectives. A detective with lustrous hair and a gun in her purse.

In ten days it would be Easter, Mary's favourite holiday. The resurrection and the life never failed to give Mary hope, as she spent the week arranging bunnies and chicks in the window of the baby store. Three days a week selling baby clothes and it was still too much pressure. She prayed for the defensive skills of Jasmine, Liz Tate, and even Joanne, who lumbered through life ignoring the daily street slang hurled at her by every group. Mary couldn't get tough. She tried to give herself an edge with her crew cut, and her thin girl's body, disciplined into hardness by hours of running on asphalt and Spartan eating. But everything that touched her bruised except the sweet gay men and tough gay women who understood the fragility beneath the leather, the motorcycles and the construction boots. They were there for a reason; to protect. Mary soothed herself, knowing that Jesus would help her, if she kept gift-wrapping copies of *Stuart Little* and musical pillows that played *Rock-a-bye Baby*. It was the beginning of Mary's second year at Toddler Togs.

Jasmine called her at the store on the Saturday before Palm Sunday. Elizabeth Tate (Jasmine always called her by her full name) had given her the keys to her house and big screen TV. Her satellite dish picked up some frequency not yet accessible to the public.

'Come with me tonight. She's got a special channel that's showing all those pre-Hayes Office Marlene Dietrich movies. Let's go watch. They're supposed to be great. She told me to be sure and invite you if you'd like to come.' Only a little of the stardust aimed at Jasmine fell on Mary, but it was enough to get her hooked. How can one be jealous, when one is nuts about the new best friend?

That night Jasmine had the same wild look from when they were kids just before the officer came up from behind to arrest them for shoplifting. Mary climbed into the garnet-red Jaguar, fastening her seatbelt as they headed up Benedict Canyon looking for trouble. The police had already arrested Elizabeth Tate for driving home drunk from Jasmine's house. Outraged, she told them the cops let her off with a warning, and an escorted drive home, but even then, Mary knew the police unwittingly controlled her ardour and panic as she lost it for Jasmine. Mary also got ticketed in front of Jasmine's house for parking in the wrong direction, which she'd done in her hurry to see them both again.

Liz Tate's house was empty. Liz was out on a date. What a move. She was present in the house without having to be there. Elizabeth Tate understood that people fall in love in movie theatres long after the actors are gone. Like instinctual physicists, actresses are some of the few people who know it's absolutely possible to be in two places at once. The great ones manage to be in three places; your theatre, your dreams, and their life. Mary had to get a grip. These were women whose goal in life was to make everyone watch them. Sexual distinction was irrelevant. It is possible to get so cynical about the packaging of celebrities, that one forgets how powerful some of them really are.

Jasmine and Mary carefully neutralised the alarm system with the code word H-A-I-R as they'd been told, and let themselves into another world.

Liz Tate did no shopping, Jasmine announced as if Liz had found the secret to life. Perhaps she had. With the casual propriety of a new best friend, Jasmine showed her the kitchen as she lit a cigarette without being too careful of the ashes. It was a territorial message. As meticulous as Mary was with her own few possessions, she admired Jasmine's more casual approach to stuff. The accoutrements weren't that important to her and never had been. One could think that money had created this attitude, but Mary remembered

Jasmine treating her first bicycle like a piece of equipment rather than a new member of the family. If she got a flat she fixed it, unlike Mary who continually watched her tyres for softness. Mary's sense of responsibility would have overwhelmed her if she had been given someone else's mansion for the evening, but Jasmine accepted the gift in a way that caught Mary's attention. Her friend was both very nervous and very confident about her power over Liz Tate.

They spent a full five minutes in front of the four-door refrigerator studying the contents. A valet service regularly picked up individual gourmet dinners specially prepared to order for Elizabeth Tate and stocked her kitchen.

Labelled entrees and vegetables stacked the shelves of the freezer ready to be zapped by the microwave. The house was a perfect setting with no particular characteristics except expensive. Pool, tennis court, landscaping, everything in order. It could have been a man's or woman's house or a company house kept for the highest echelon for entertaining or corporate use. Only the photos of Elizabeth with her dogs, Elizabeth playing polo, Elizabeth looking adorable, indicated that anyone lived there.

While they sat in the dark watching the big screen TV, Mary knew she was only along for the ride as Jasmine chain-smoked and brooded. Mary couldn't read her friend, tonight the actress whose composed face masked what she was really feeling.

Nothing happened; they had her house but no Liz Tate. She had performed the ultimate actress's trick. Her audience could think of no one else, and she wasn't even there. After the show, where Marlene Dietrich, like a witch doctor with literal smoke and feathers, absolutely convinced them she was the most desirable woman on the face of the earth, they locked up and drove home. Jasmine dropped Mary off, and her apartment, sparse and lean with almost no possessions, seemed alive and real. Mary felt more solid than she had in a long time.

· *Six* ·

'Mary, doll, I got seven boxes,' yelled Jimmy, the UPS man, as he stopped the truck inches from the back door of the store.

'Seven boxes. Shit, Jimmy, seven.'

'Two boxes are small.'

'It's baby clothes, Jimmy. Do you know how many baby clothes you can get in a small box?'

'You know Mondays. They stack up over the weekend.'

On this Monday, Mary liked looking into the totally honest face of the UPS man. After the complexity of the weekend, it was a relief to watch the moves of a man who could only be in one place at a time. Mary always liked him and knew he was honest for two reasons. One, he was stupid as dirt, and two he was good. Today these qualities, so boring on every other Monday, gave him an appeal and sincerity, combined with a very solid forearm and shoulder muscle, that interested Mary in prolonging the conversation a little.

'Monday's a big day, huh?'

'Killer. After Monday, the rest of the week is a piece of pie.'

'Lugging those boxes around keeps you in shape, Jimmy.'

'Does it? Do I look OK, Mary? You know I just turned forty, no wife, no kids, I don't know.'

'You look good, Jimmy.'

She wasn't lying. He was a real Jimmy. His kid's name suited him and she saw why it stuck, as he jumped back into the truck throwing the stick shift into reverse with the ease of a great driver. She saw him understanding how the gears worked, and why the engine ignited, and the balance of the clutch and accelerator. Cars and trucks were it for Jimmy, that much was clear. It occurred to her that maybe he was smart in another way; a literal, mechanical way that could fix machines and read maps.

'Hey, maybe we could eat together after work sometime,' he yelled in her direction, too shy to wait for an answer.

Out of the question, her brain told her, trying to dominate the other tiny voice that said, 'Yeah, maybe sometime, Jimmy.'

She took the mat knife and sliced open the first of seven boxes. 200 Oshkosh overalls needed 800 straight pins removed, 400 labels cut off, and 200 pieces of tissue thrown away, before steaming. It was an afternoon's work made for daydreaming as her thoughts wandered from Jimmy to Debra, a temptress with a trail of boys behind her. Debra

73

wanted to give her a free massage one night after work.

Life was getting too sexy. Mary called Raymond during a break. A nice meal and his sexual clarity would cool things down.

'Darling, a UPS man, talk to me.' Raymond was marinating a piece of flank steak in balsamic vinegar, red wine, oregano, and masses of black pepper and garlic.

'From now on it's garlic on everything. On cereal in the morning. They say it's stronger than penicillin. What have I got to lose? AZT is a joke.' Raymond, pumped up to manly perfection by a trainer three times a week at the gym, had been diagnosed HIV positive.

Except for a permanent purple bruise on his wrist that looked innocent enough, but hid a tumour like an iceberg hides it's size, he could have posed for the cover of a New Age magazine as an extreme example of physically fit good health.

Within seconds, limits had been set on every future word and action. All the rituals of their friendship stayed exactly the same; they just happened a shade faster. Mary doubted she would ever get her friend back as hysteria invaded his personality. There was no slowing him down as he tried to run from the disease even in his sleep. The night his lover died, she sat on a chair in his bedroom, watching Raymond try to nap with the same energy it takes to run a marathon. The two young men from the mortuary quickly removed the body from the apartment, pulling out the needle to the morphine drip which eased the lover's last three days. Raymond and Mary had seen so much death, they took it for granted that after the final request for morphine, three days was all that was left. They'd never seen a friend come back from the morphine drip.

It was a young knowledge of death they couldn't explain to parents. There was no element of surprise that could link them to their father's and mother's experience with war death. It was slow and manifested itself differently in every friend. This lover died in his brain, never losing his weight or his looks, just his faculties. Mary became Margie and Raymond became Richard, as the memory connections broke down. He gave up quickly.

Others fought through every stage, losing the looks and the hair and everything but the bone, the anger, and the spirituality. But the morphine drip signalled the end. Just the words carried a weight and significance that turned every watching friend into an expert.

But they couldn't talk about it twenty-four hours a day, so they kept returning to their happy sexual chatter and cooking.

'So Jimmy's built. I spend a fortune at the gym. He throws a few boxes around, gets paid for it, and looks fabulous.'

'He doesn't look as good as you.'

'Honey, if he can make that awful brown UPS uniform work, he'll look like a million in real clothes.'

'You're right.'

'Of course I'm right. Put a Fedex man or a UPS man in jeans, and it's a whole other ball game. Postman's outfits are a tiny bit better. The stripe on the pants shows a little flair. Oh God, I should be designing. Of course the policemen look the best. And I don't even want to go into the firemen. Here in L.A. they all look like movie stars. I mean better than movie stars. Bigger. Let's light a small kitchen grease fire and see what comes to save us.'

'OK. But after we've eaten. Is it almost ready?'

'Not yet. Eat some cookies.'

They always ate out of sequence. Away from home for years, and it still gave them secret pleasure to eat dessert before dinner.

Close to midnight, after hours of listening to CDs programmed to repeat their favourite songs, Mary drove home. For the moment they gave their tears to Barbra Streisand and Dusty Springfield. Nothing seemed that important, until Mary saw Joanne; her gorilla walk unmistakable even in the shadows as she lurched down Franklin Avenue. Mary pulled up along side.

'Hey, Joanne, how are you doing?'

'Fuck, Mary, my car broke down.'

'What a nightmare. Get in, I'll take you home.'

'Okay, but, hey, I don't owe you anything. You know what I'm saying.'

'Jesus, Joanne, that's why I'm out this late. I'm looking to rape someone in the bushes on Franklin Avenue.'

'Yeah, yeah, I just want to get things straight.' Mary liked that Joanne always thought she was

76

about to pounce. It made her happy that somewhere Joanne knew she was irresistible, although in point of fact Mary had long abandoned any sexual designs on her independent friend.

'Why are you out this late?' Now that things were settled, Joanne grudgingly got into the car.

'Raymond's HIV positive. He started to cry tonight. We looked at magazines and played our favourite music until he stopped. It took a long time.'

'I'm so sorry. Please give him my love.' Joanne turned articulate and womanly with the tragic news.

'Come upstairs, Mary. I'll make some tea and I have Japanese cookies.'

Mary exhaled after holding her breath for three hours. They climbed the stairs and Mary immediately saw a new painting on the living room wall.

'That's me!' Mary pointed to the painting of herself hanging out of a car window. The car was orange, drawn in a hard realistic style and Mary, the image, smiled, looking straight at the observer like the Mona Lisa. Sunglasses hid the eyes.

'Yeah, well, I took that photo of you and I liked it, so I made a painting. Nobody chases me like you do, Mary. Nobody takes me to plays and concerts. I met Raymond. You introduce me to your friends like you're proud to know me.'

'I am.'

'I know. But I outweigh you by about a hundred pounds. You and I both know it wouldn't work. I'm queer. I've known since I was six in the foster home. All I've ever wanted was a woman to love

77

me. But you, you still look at guys. You don't think you do, but I see it.'

'No, that's over for me.'

'I don't think so. You're pretty. If you let your hair grow, you've got those curls. Look, I put them in the painting. Guys look at you. I see that too. Since Heather, you don't notice. She blinded both of us, but I have more experience with these things. Eat a cookie, they're real expensive. No sugar. Just rice juice or something.'

'Mmmm. They're good.'

They sat for a minute savouring the shiny Japanese cookies. Raymond's contagious hysteria ebbed a little, as Mary let herself be soothed by the tea and Joanne's understanding.

· *Seven* ·

On Good Friday, Mary was quite content to be
steaming hundreds of pairs of tiny lederhosen,
when the phone rang. It was Jasmine. 'Come
straight from work,' she said, 'Elizabeth Tate
is already here.' Mary was wearing her uniform
covered with tiny seals with balls on their noses.
She thought it was an appropriate look for the store,
but felt a little insecure about chaperoning the two
femme fatales looking like Popo the Clown.

Jasmine jumped up from the kitchen table and
grabbed Mary's arm as she came in the back door.
It was not a casual touch, she was holding on.
Elizabeth Tate sat at the kitchen table seriously
loosening up. After years of living with a mother
who panicked easily, Mary knew how to become
steady in the midst of hysteria. She stayed quiet,
Jasmine calmed down and seemed so happy to
see her, Mary breathed with relief. She knew
Jasmine was using her to dilute the intensity of
the magnetism between her and Liz, but she made

it clear that Mary was home base. In the presence of the fabulous Liz Tate, Mary wasn't feeling too important, as she watched the two of them pull into each other.

But the seduction included Mary too; she told herself anyway. How many lies are possible in the presence of glamorous women? Men know this. Now it was Mary's turn to learn. Out of her mind with loneliness in this sparkling group, she tugged at her baggy pants. But they looked at her with such good humour when she did her stupid clown outfit jokes, that Mary allowed herself to be swept along into the weekend.

'Do you know how many people in the world I could be spending Easter with?' Elizabeth asked repeatedly. It was not so much bragging, as disbelief at where she'd found herself. Jasmine's husband was out of town, so it was just the girls ready to roll. They were drinking at the kitchen table, as Mary took a soda from the fridge. She needed a cool head for these two.

Mary mentioned to Jasmine that Raymond was HIV positive. The room went quiet, until Liz Tate told them her hairdresser had just died.

'Soon there won't be any gay hairdressers alive in this city. We're all going to look like shit,' she said. The girls knew her comment was just show business bullshit to cover how much she missed her real best friend, the man who made her beautiful.

Elizabeth zoomed up from the table suddenly having to get something out of her car; the navy blue Jaguar sort of parked three feet from the curb in front of the house.

'She's nice, isn't she?' Jasmine asked looking for confirmation. Nice wasn't the first word that came to Mary's mind but she nodded. Elizabeth Tate came back from the car with a baby blue cosmetics case.

'This is what I need,' she said as she snapped the locks of the three-tiered display of sun-protected brown prescription bottles. The suitcase was filled with drugs. Liz always carried a full pharmacy with her, just in case she got a cold, or a headache, or an undesirable feeling of any kind.

'This is nothing. You should see Liza Minelli's.' Mary laughed and knew exactly where she was coming from. Elizabeth was still A.O.K. in her book. Mary understood people who had to feel perfect bordering on sublime twenty-four hours a day. Her first addict-love was Gretta, who came out of a nod in the Hollywood YWCA sauna, to say something really funny about once a month. Mary thought she was so quiet and deep, and then inspired with a childlike gaiety when she put her underpants on her head. Finally Gretta's sweating girlfriend broke Mary's trance when she looked at her point blank and said, 'It's not depth, it's heroin.'

Elizabeth tossed back a pill without bothering to explain it's use. The actresses were now vibrating on exactly the same frequency. Mary could see their bodies quiver with sensitivity to each other, responding in a way that was too fast to follow. Mary trembled that way the night she lost her virginity. Suddenly, Liz was hungry and wanted to eat, so they all threw on a little make-up, and hit the streets in Mary's car. With two Jaguars parked outside, they still decided on Mary's Corolla. Stoned out of her mind, Elizabeth knew how to protect the body that brought home the bacon.

Only Mary consciously knew that dinner was Liz Tate's way of sidetracking her frenzied libido before the drugs kicked in. Jasmine stayed cool. She was wearing a short blue madras shift from the sixties that worked in the nineties. As always Liz wore neutral, nondescript clothes that didn't distract from her natural beauty. She didn't need decoration. And Mary looked like she was about to make an appearance on *Captain Kangaroo*.

Thrifty Drug was the first stop. Liz needed a prescription filled. She warned they'd better make it quick or they'd be mobbed. As glamorous as the company was, Mary privately doubted the fan fervour of the six Koreans in the Gower Gulch Thrifty. They managed to escape relatively unnoticed, although Liz was in such a state about being recognized they caught some attention just because they were so disruptive. Dashing next door into a big, cheap Japanese restaurant, Liz was recognized immediately. She relaxed a bit when her fame was confirmed. They asked for a dark table in the back room and the two beauties settled themselves next to each other on the banquette and Mary sat opposite.

Everything was too loud, too manic, and too stimulating. Mary couldn't hold her own, and was afraid of being swept away into their careless world, where cash could buy off speeding tickets and clean up any casual mistake. One could burn down a house or get arrested and the most serious consequence would be bad publicity. Mary didn't want to be in that world with no money. It could be dangerous. She was miserable. The girls were lost in each other and Mary was doing the driving. She longed to compete, unhappy with herself and her perceived failure. There was that. Then there was the more humdrum jealousy of shared friendship. From far away behind her own protective walls, Mary observed that Jasmine and Elizabeth were giving off light. She knew about the easy crushes of actors, but forgot in the presence of its effervescent power.

The couple next to them celebrated a birthday, and when Elizabeth Tate joined in on the song, their eyes bugged and they asked the girls to pose for Polaroids. 'Aren't you famous, too?' they asked Jasmine. Then they asked Mary, who felt stupid, but Elizabeth insisted she pose for a picture. Liz Tate was having a great old time. Mary figured that years later the couple's children would look at the picture and be impressed by the stars and the fact that their parents had hired a lady clown to entertain at the party.

After this burst of goodwill, the energy dropped from brilliant to merely bright. They inhaled dinner, which they didn't have to pay for, compliments of the house, climbed into Mary's car, and headed for Jasmine's.

In the clarity of non-verbal communication, it had been decided they were spending the night. Jasmine played mother and gave them nightgowns. Nightgowns she accumulated from scenes played in the big-budget horror movies that marked her early career. The heroine/victim of these movies is at her most vulnerable and exposed and beautiful in the bedroom, so these gowns were really something. If the forces of evil should blow open the bedroom shutters, the gowns billowed revealing even more of our terrified girl. Liz wore peach, Jasmine wore mint green, and Mary had the baby blue.

They looked like mermaids as they gathered in the middle guest room. This was Elizabeth's room, connected to Mary's through a small bathroom and just down the hall from Jasmine's. The room was country innocent, with dormer windows, a braided rug on the floor, and an antique quilt on the bed. Jasmine grabbed a pillow and stretched out on the rug, her arms behind her head, playing the vamp. Liz, on the bed, fussing with her cosmetics case, decided which pill would be perfect.

'I want to calm down, but I don't want to sleep, but I want to sleep eventually, but I don't want a hangover. I wish Liza was here, she would know exactly what to take. It's like being with a doctor.'

Mary fiddled with the tape deck and tried to find the perfect song. She was curious about the sexuality that was potent in the room. What happens at a slumber party when the girls are over thirty, and their hair already looks great?

Jasmine was all passive female availability lying on the rug in a sheer gown with no underwear. What was the message, Mary wondered. She was, of course, showing off how beautiful she was, that went without saying. She was an actress, and underneath the private lifestyle was the required streak of physical exhibitionism. Or was she just being normal, casual about her body around friends of her own sex, and Mary was the introverted, shy one aware of her bare shoulders and the intimacy of three half naked women in a small bedroom? Or was Jasmine doing that thing girls do, which is show their girlfriends how sexy they are when men aren't around?

Mary found the song. She wanted to play *Lover Man (Oh Where Can You Be)* on Linda Ronstadt's *What's New* album but settled on *I Don't Stand A Ghost Of A Chance With You*. She wasn't part of the situation so at least she could comment on it. Her sense of humour was trying to save her.

The girls settled a little as she played the old–fashioned music as background to their fantasies. Mary knew exactly what Elizabeth Tate was doing. On that night, fluffy and dressed to kill or be killed, Liz was going to do one of two things. She was either going to get stoned enough to make a pass at Jasmine, or stoned enough to forget she ever felt such a desire.

Mary had knowledge from another part of town where people acted on these passing lusts, and she tried to look lovely as she hated herself for having sexualized friendship. It was exhausting to feel

85

sexual tension with everyone. There was no place to rest.

The energy had been so high that a kind of numbness set in. With no acceptable target for the sexuality in the room, the girls went blank. Jasmine and Elizabeth had prolonged the tease beyond its peak and didn't know what to do. If a husband or boyfriend had appeared, he would have been eaten alive. But as it was, they'd reached a stalemate.

Mary was getting tired in a hyper kind of way, afraid to miss something but winding down, so she took the tape deck and provisionally went back to her room. Her exit seemed to finish off the evening and Jasmine primly said goodnight. Since their rooms were connected, Mary heard Elizabeth fussing with her pills and mumbling to herself. It was going to take more than drugs and lights out to dim that energy. She sounded like a squirrel in the walls, squeaking and scratching.

Elizabeth was her body and senses primarily. Most people rely on clothes to further define and enhance their identity. But Liz's clothes had no particular style and didn't even fit well, like she hadn't had time to try them on before buying. Mary was sure they were expensive, but they looked like the most generic slacks, blouses and shoes in the Sears catalogue. Mary suspected that most of Liz's possessions were bought for her by strangers. The effect was an orphaned, helpless look on a woman who could drill the bad guys at fifty paces. She combined stereotypes and gender symbols with an artist's eye, and turned herself into something original.

The whole world agreed that Liz Tate was fabulous. Maybe not in Brazil or sections of Africa, but millions of little girls emulated her and millions of men desired her, so Mary quickly dismissed any feeling she had as the part of her that responds to pop figures the same way everybody else does.

But still, she was intrigued by her thinness, her breathy voice, her fragility, and the boy inside the girl. In the second grade Mary had a boy inside of her. He liked to climb trees and play with a ball and a knife and even take a punch once in a while to be a hero. He liked to belong to a gang and think his gang was the best. He loved exploring and microscopes and anything to do with cowboys except cowgirls.

Jasmine had a boy inside of her too. Mary knew it the first day they met, but Jasmine frilled up over the years and probably forgot about him. Mary wished she could forget about her boy. But someone like Liz Tate made her remember that so much is just a pretty act that keeps the boy-girls acceptable in the world. And when a boy-girl turns into a delicate, small-boned lovely woman, the boys love her and the girls love her, and everyone is fooled, including the boy-girl who doesn't know what the fuck is going on. This is what Mary was thinking about as she went to sleep.

In the middle of the night a crash shook the walls of Mary's room, and she woke up. She heard a very quiet repressed moan and then Liz Tate called her name. Mary. Not Jasmine's name, her name. That was Mary's first awareness.

Mary raced through the bathroom in the dark and found Liz kneeling next to the wall in her room. She'd walked smack into it. Suddenly it was okay to touch Elizabeth Tate.

'It's OK, it's OK,' Mary said holding her shoulders strong. The touch was right, and Liz put her arm around Mary's waist. They both got quiet and steady as Mary carefully felt her face and head for blood.

They were very close for a long scientific minute probing and testing for swelling or damage. Mary wondered why she called her. Her practical self voiced all the logical reasons; she was near, she'd been the chaperone all weekend, she didn't want to bother Jasmine. Then again, maybe Liz Tate knew Mary was a boy-girl too and discerned the hidden part of her that loved machines and running and cool boy clothes and hated dolls and carriages and being still.

'Don't turn on the light, Mary. I can't believe I did this. I really hurt my head. Swear you won't tell anyone. Oh God, my head hurts.'

Mary was a fabulous nurse. No hint of a tremble tipped her hand and her heart beat steady as she checked for broken skin. No doctor was going to see this wound, she was pretty sure.

Jasmine turned on the hall light, realised what happened in one second and took immediate control of the situation. She was a whirlwind of ice packs and efficiency and Mary was quickly not part of what

88

was going on. They were a couple and Mary was the facilitator, until the accident. Then the accident took over and Florence Nightingale approved every intimacy.

Mary was getting so goddamned sick of these girls.

Elizabeth had walked into a wall to get Jasmine to play doctor. Unnoticed, Mary went back to her room, as the murmurings and comfortings continued. Whatever their nature, she was out of it.

Until Liz Tate, nothing had ever made her feel competitive with Jasmine. Not the recreational sports, not the money or the adoration, not even her husband Peter, who, with two hit scripts to his credit, was considered a catch in Hollywood. Quite the contrary, Mary and Peter joked together like siblings, easily understanding each other's regard for Jasmine. But this was a horse of a different colour. Something about these girl games hurt Mary. They weren't direct and nobody told the truth. How could they? No one understood the subject, no matter how many times everyone said it was the nineties.

In confusion, Mary called Joanne, who set her straight. 'Forget about Liz Tate. She's a hit and run. The worst. They disappear and everybody left needs hospitalization. The hotter she is for Jasmine, the quicker she'll marry some guy with a big P.R. wedding to convince herself that girls don't mean shit. She'll play homemaker for a year, lay off the drugs, and split when she can't take it anymore.

Then it's his turn to stand around with his dick in his hands. You can be sure your friend doesn't know what hit her either.'

What a comfort. It occurred to Mary that her wounds might force her back into a cautious truce with the opposite sex. It was familiar ground where she understood the rules, even if she didn't like them. But after ten minutes of this idea, she rejected it. Just because she had a few scratches didn't mean the men were going to turn into the good guys.

· *Eight* ·

Debra first wandered into the store dressed in a sheer black blouse, no bra, mustard tights and matching Robin Hood boots. This was not the usual look for a baby store matron, who generally wore a floral print Villager blouse, canvas wrap-around skirt, espadrilles and real pearls. Mary's neutered appearance somehow suited the store, suggesting Peter Pan or some renegade fairy from a gentle English children's tale. Toddlers stopped crying the minute they saw Mary, and for this the mothers loved her. Mrs Daladier, a regular customer, broke the formal sales relationship when she asked if Mary was free to babysit for her four blond boys.

'They like you, and they don't just like everybody,' Mrs Daladier told her as she offered to pay her and feed her the following Saturday night.

Mary watched Debra finger the less conservative, trendy items hanging on the centre rack. She kept staring at Mary who figured her for a shoplifter, the scrutiny was so intense. Finally she asked for help with a Christening gift for a baby girl. Mary, the professional, avoided the eyes and semi-exposed breasts of this beauty as she pointed out the infant pink and white sleepers.

'Do you have anything in black? I want something different.'

'It's hard to find anything in black for infants.' Mary said seriously trying to give the impression of thinking.

'I know it's weird, but this kid's from the Addams Family I swear to God. The mother's a performance artist. She nurses the baby onstage, while the husband beats a single drum and howls. My gift has to make a statement.'

'I guess a *Rock-a-Bye Baby* pillow is out of the question.' Debra laughed. Bingo, they connected.

'Actually, I do have a little harlequin sleeper in purple and red. It's the most radical thing we sell for infants. What do you think?'

'Not bad. That might work. Good, I'll take it.'

Mary gift-wrapped the present, processed the gold Visa card, and gave Debra her package.

'Listen, thanks for your help. Here's my card. If you ever need a massage, call me.'

Okey-dokey thought Mary, as she watched Debra toss her hair with deliberate flirtatious intent. Stop it, she told herself, as she decided the hair toss was just a mannerism and anything more was a wishful fantasy. But Mary kept the card.

She looked forward to the evening. Mrs Daladier's offer to babysit and Debra's flirting left her drained.

Too much pressure. Mary lined up a night of TV. Charles Bronson on Channel Five at eight o'clock made it a perfect plan. After Charles, she'd watch a little public access to catch up on the latest spiritual trends, and sleep for ten hours.

Three phone calls interrupted her isolation. One was Lawrence, one was Debra, and one was Elizabeth Tate. Lawrence, the pest, had an uncanny way of calling whenever Mary entertained the occasional male fantasy. He beamed in on some channel she was trying to keep quiet. Charles Bronson turned it on this night with his hard body and sad face.

'Mary, what's up?'

'You called me, Lawrence. What's up with you?' she said, not giving him a break.

He overlooked her tone and continued. 'Well, what about that dinner we discussed, and *Rocky IV*?'

'I work nights now. I babysit.'

'Every night. Every single night?'

'Yes.'

'Oh. Well, how about this idea? You call me. Anytime you get off, I'm available. What could be easier?'

Mary had to soften. Nothing fazed him, not her severe tone, not her rejection, not her obvious excuses. She knew about asking women out on dates, and she knew how hard it was to face the instant change in the voice as they were too busy, too tired, or too uninterested. No matter how nicely it was done, how much they wanted to be friends, it was clearly get out of my face.

93

'All right, Lawrence, I will, I promise. How are things going?'

'I'm making so much money I don't know what to do with it. The business runs itself and I just won 600 beans at the track. I'm looking at a new condo, two floors and a deck. $300,000, what do I care, I'm not putting anybody through college. I like a nice place, you know. I like it clean, I like it neat. I'm breaking my balls here, and for what, unless I live right, you know what I mean. I like to live right. And I like some pussy every once in a while. Is something wrong with this? I ain't married. You, I like There's something about you. You're a clean girl. You know. Give me a holler some time. I won't jump on you till after dinner. Just kidding, just kidding.'

He was hard to resist, once he got on a roll. Mary was laughing and watching Charles Bronson with no sound, as call waiting kicked in.

'Hey, Lawrence, I have to go. We'll talk, I promise. Have a good night.' She pressed the phone button transferring to the other call.

'Hi,' said the sultriest female voice in the world. 'I got your number through the store manager. I hope you don't mind. It's Debra from today.'

Debra. Oh boy, front and centre. Mary sat up in her bed and instantly decided her flannel sheets would have to go.

'They don't give out home numbers.'

'I said I was a lawyer and one of your more distant cousins left you something in his will. People always respond to found money. They gave me your number right away. You know, you've got a great sense of humour. I needed a few laughs so I thought I'd call.'

Charles Bronson and Lawrence both made direct-ness a very attractive quality just moments ago, so Mary was in no mood for girl games as she reacted to Debra's detective work. It was easy to be brave when Debra's awesome physical presence wasn't standing in front of her driving every rational thought out of her head. That made it easier for Mary to call a spade a spade.

'Well, I'm flattered. That's nice, but I think I'd better tell you right off I date women. And most nice straight ladies don't want me for a girlfriend once they find out. There are exceptions, but they're very clear about who they are. Do you understand what I'm saying?'

Debra didn't falter as she whispered into the phone, 'Mary, thank you for trusting me enough to be honest. Some of my best friends live with women. They're so strong, they empower me. Personally I'm normal, I'm just looking for a husband actually, but in the meantime I have to earn a living, and I just graduated from massage school. All the practice subjects are fat, and when I saw you being sweet with the kids and funny with me, I figured you weren't an axe murderer, and I could practice massage on your thin body. You'd be doing me a favour.'

Put this in a movie and nobody would buy it, Mary thought as she sifted through the unintended insults in Debra's proposal. 'Empower' was annoying, 'normal' was tough, but Mary's skin was getting thicker as she backed off from a confrontation.

The unexpressed tirade went through Mary's brain anyway. 'Axe murderer, guess again, cookie. Empower you, how about embitter me and some of your other goddamn best friends. What the hell are you doing, walking around half naked in the afternoon, you goddamn Hollywood flake, offering free massages? Who's kidding who here?' The fury came strong, because Mary was weakening. This gorgeous number, at least ten years younger, was pursuing her, no matter how much she said she wanted that husband.

'Listen, sweetie,' Debra sighed. 'I have a table at the Academy of the Body Arts and Sciences. It's not my apartment. It's a classroom. You bring the oil of your choice. The teacher will be there. He may even work on you.'

Mary lost.

'OK, where do I go?'

Debra gave her some address in Santa Monica and breathed 'sleep well' into the phone. Mary switched the TV over to some new guru talking really, really fast about serenity and peace. She muted the sound and watched him bob up and down, as the telephone rang for the third and final time.

'Mary, it's Liz Tate. How are you?'

'Fine, Liz, how's your head doing?' Mary asked casually. Liz wasn't the only actress in the world, as Mary's heart threatened to jump through the roof.

'I had a hell of a goose egg, but I took an anti-inflammatory pill that brought it right down. Listen, I called to ask you about Jasmine. You've known her for a long time, right?'

'Since we were seven years old.'

'Does she know how adorable she is?'

Just chitchat. Just the lightest form of flattery, like telling a friend her outfit is cute.

'Well, she's having a lot of success in the movies but underneath I think she has her doubts, like anybody else.' Mary always shifted into neutral when people asked her about Jasmine. Her loyalty, though shaken, wanted to stay absolute. She needed the ideal of a best friend, even if the reality had slipped. In Hollywood, there was always the possibility that an idealised image could save them.

'What's her husband like?' Light as a feather, like asking for the salt or butter.

'Peter's great. He's very talented. They adore each other.'

'So it's a good marriage?'

'Solid as a rock.'

'That's pretty rare in this town. My track record's shit. What does Jasmine see in men anyway?' Just girl talk. Liz Tate gave away no secrets.

'Do you want to know the real answer to that question?'

'Shoot.'

'She likes their chests.'

'That can't be the whole thing.'

'It is. With Peter, it's much deeper, naturally, but on the generic level, the thing that keeps her going with men is their chests. It's not that complicated.'

They laughed. It wasn't a bad reason. It was as good as some guy liking their tits.

'I keep trying,' Liz explained, 'but underneath the bullshit, all they want to do is take my money. The agents, the lawyers, the husbands, my own father, for Christ's sake. He's a goddamn cracker living in a mansion I paid for in Mississippi. He's such a hick, he's lucky if his piss hits the bowl. Before I got famous, he used a hole in the ground. Now that Mom's dead, he'd like me to stay home and cut eye-holes in the sheets for the cross burnings on Saturday nights. And my ex doesn't even try to look for work after the settlement I gave him. On a really hard day, he waxes the surfboard. And I'm supposed to enjoy sucking their cocks? Who's kidding who, here? If I could find one thing to like, I'd be so happy.'

Words failed Mary, not that it mattered. Liz kept talking. 'I really understand why all those girls fall in love with convicts. I mean, no problem, the guys are in jail and the girls can talk to their girlfriends all day about being in love. I think I'll get me a convict. Some guy on death row who I'm rehabilitating with my love letters. He'll hit the gas chamber, I'll break down and ride the publicity wave for two years. What do you think, Mary?'

'Sounds good to me.'

'I've been married three times in two years. I've got to do something different.'

'Well, you work so hard, it must be difficult.'
Stroke, stroke, stroke. Keep Liz talking about
herself. Despite the jokes and perfect acting, Mary
knew Liz was madly in love with Jasmine, and
having a lonely time in her big movie star house.
The phone call alone was evidence of Liz's need.

'You were great in *The Girl Team*. I mean you
gave little girls hope. I used to hear them talking
at the newsstand back home, when you made all
the covers that first time. God, they thought you
were the coolest.'

'Did they? I was working so hard, I didn't have
much contact with anybody in the real world.
You know if you ever want to barbecue or swim
or anything, please feel free to use the house. Just
call Selena, the housekeeper. I'll put you on the list.'

'Thanks Liz. I appreciate it. I'll never forget
Easter.'

'When you see Jasmine, tell her we talked.
She must be out of town. I keep getting her
machine.'

'She's shooting *Demon Changeling Boy II* in
Denver. It's hard to keep up with that girl.'
Mary gave Liz the information she wanted. Movie
productions and contact numbers were listed in the
trade papers anyway. It was time for Jasmine to
run her own interference. This was bordering on
masochism.

'Thanks, Mary. Goodbye.'

Sleep took its time as Mary tried to figure
out her sudden popularity. She refocused on
Bronson. Boy, was he aging well, she thought

99

as she drifted off into a dreamland of martial arts and Tai Chi kicks. Charlie could protect her from the bad guys anytime. But would he know a bad girl if she walked right up and spit in his face?

· *Nine* ·

Mary carefully shaved her legs in the bathtub, preparing her body for Debra's massage. The yearly doctor's checkup didn't get this kind of presentation as she even shaved the three or four tiny hairs off her big toe.

She drove herself through Hollywood traffic, and Beverly Hills, past Century City into the mellower vibes of Santa Monica. On the second floor of a corner mini mall, she saw the storefront Academy of Body Arts and Sciences next to a Tanning Plus on one side and a Supercuts Salon on the other. For this occasion, Debra had chosen to wear thongs providing more coverage for her feet than the shorts and halter top she was wearing on her body. There was a six inch space between the fabric of her shorts and halter just grazing the bottom of her major breasts swinging loose again without a bra.

This is some kind of test was the only thought passing through Mary's head as she tried to close down all her senses and act casual.

'Hi.' Again the Marilyn Monroe voice. 'I thought more students would be here. It's usually full on a Friday night, but it's just you, me and Paul.'

The Academy of Body Arts and Sciences was a large dimly lit room with two rows of gurney-like tables, not unlike an emergency ward of a hospital. There were a few charts of the human body hanging on the walls, and a little cluster of diplomas certifying the scientific nature of the work they were about to do.

'This is Paul.'

'How do you do, Paul?' Mary thought a little formality was called for as Paul tried to keep his tongue in and the drool from actually running down his chin as Debra took his arm and pressed it against her breasts.

Paul wasn't really a sleazy guy. Like Mary, he was Debra's hostage, trying to present a reasonably controlled human male as she played an advanced game of 'look, but don't touch'. His body was tiny, all tendons and bone, and his eyes had the buggy, clear look of too many vitamins and not enough food. Mary remembered the look from the kids who went on the brown rice diet in the seventies. They appeared totally healthy until they got hepatitis and had to be hospitalized for six months.

Paul was Debra's slave as she whispered into his ear, 'Tell us about protein, Paul.'

'You can get all the protein you need from peas.'

'Just peas?' Mary grasped at nutrition; any topic to reroute the libido.

'Absolutely. I'm a complete vegetarian. I don't eat animals or any animal products. No eggs, no cheese, no dairy, just peas for protein.' Paul looked like he could drop dead at any moment, and they were in very flattering light.

'Take off your clothes and wrap yourself in this.' Debra handed Mary a microscopic towel. Mary withdrew to the changing room. She badly needed a massage from the tension of trying to relax for the massage.

Actual lovers had not been as overtly sexual as Debra seemed to be during the next hour. While clinically avoiding the specific erogenous areas, she rubbed and cooed and kept her breasts millimetres from Mary's face, while occasionally resting her hand for long moments on Mary's towel covered rear end. Had Mary not spelled out her sexual history there could be some interpretation of innocence, but something else was going on and Mary wasn't quite sure what it was.

Paul stood by, but Mary knew he was too weak to be a threat. He was a looker, nothing more, and Debra's teasing fulfilled his every fantasy. Paul's torture was not over, as Debra held his little body against her hip while Mary changed after the massage. They wanted her to go for Chinese food, but no meat and another hour of Debra's heavy-lidded non-pursuit was impossible. Mary waved goodbye and escaped to her car, driving quickly back to Hollywood and the true degenerates who left her alone.

The minute she got home, Mary called Joanne,

who picked up on the first half ring. 'Joanne, can I come over? I need someone to talk to.'

'Just talk, no funny business, you know what I mean.'

'Joanne, for God's sake, haven't we cleared this up?'

'Yeah, well, I don't want any surprises. I lost a couple of pounds. I look good.'

'I swear I won't make a pass at you.'

Mary pulled into the alley, and Joanne buzzed her in. 'Boy, you look pretty, Joanne. It's a good thing I promised. What did you lose, about ten pounds?'

'Yeah.' Joanne turned away to hide the first smile Mary had ever seen on her anguished face, and added, 'Don't get any ideas.'

'You're making it tough.' Again Joanne smiled and turned away.

'Want tea?'

'Yes, thank you.'

'You're so polite, Mary.'

'Joanne, this straight girl is all over me. She says she wants to be my friend. She knows I see women. I told her right away. I think it turned her on. She told me the most erotic scene she'd ever seen in a movie was between two women. Then she tells me she's hunting for a husband. And she's a looker. Men go nuts around her. Her tits are out there, you know what I mean, but expensive.'

'You're pussy-whipped,' Joanne paused with worldly contempt. 'You're so stupid. I can't believe

I feel protective toward you. She'll never sleep with you. There's a group of women. The minute they find out you've slept with a woman, they get curious. And why not. But most of the time maybe their boyfriend isn't so great, maybe they're frigid, maybe they don't like men. I don't know. They get very seductive. And sometimes they treat you like a man, if you'll notice, but they're playing. They're, what's that expression, passive something?'

'Passive–aggressive.'

'Yeah, the worst. They want you to do it all. The men know. It's another form of cock teasing. Mary, it's not worth it, unless it's true love.'

'Oh.'

'Yeah, I know what you mean. It's rough.'

'Heather was like that in a way, except she wanted sex.'

'But she would have stopped wanting after a while. That's why she jumps from girl to girl. She's looking for a female husband.'

'I heard she found a new one.'

'Who?'

'Some writer named Felicity.'

'I still feel burned.'

'Me too. How's the painting going?'

'Nothing. I'm working on this big job for United Artists. The receptionist literally shudders when I walk by. They've got me in the basement this time.'

'Oh, Joanne.'

'It's true.'

'If I wasn't a flyweight, I'd take you on.'

'I know.' The third smile of the evening lit up the room.

'See you, Joanne.'

'Yeah.'

· *Ten* ·

It took a little dancing to get out of the 'will' question at work. The store manager had been waiting all weekend to hear what Mary had inherited. 'Just some old sentimental letters' ruined the other salesgirl's day. Martha wanted to hear rags to riches, trust fund, jewellery, silver, but the fantasy lay there as they decided to refold the toddler two, toddler three, and toddler four T-shirts. There were 500 of them. Martha and Mary sat at the kiddie table and went to work. The unfortunate pairing of Martha and Mary gave rise to many religious allusions particularly around Easter time. Martha lived in a Presbyterian frenzy of good works and sweetness. Mary suspected she owed Martha her job. The more pathetic Mary appeared, the more compassionate Martha became. Her goodness was fused with lessons, however, and Mary became a ripe subject for conversion.

'I'm a Protestant already,' Mary protested when Martha wanted her to come to church to pray for longer hair. It was a reasonable request. Mary's haircut still wasn't a cute punk coif. She looked like a concentration camp victim with a single wave of curls allowed to grow over one eye. Little scissor marks still showed skin in some places. Martha decided to save Mary when she hired her on. Mary never turned down mothering of any kind, so she humoured Martha's rigorous conservative devotion.

Martha was in the middle of telling a thinly veiled allegorical story of the woman who cleaned Jesus' feet with her long hair, when Debra strolled in. There was a lot of space between the design of Debra's white lace body suit. No underwear, a seven-inch white jersey skirt and gold pumps pushed her body into the stratosphere of advertised availability.

'Debra, what's up?' Mary asked, walking to the front of the store.

'Wasn't Friday night great? I got so much energy back from working on your body. I just sucked up your vibes through my hands. Do you realise how strong your electromagnetic field is?'

'Is there something you'd like to see in a sleeper?' Mary asked, indicating the other salesgirl with a jerk of her head. She hoped Debra was grounded enough to see physical behaviour.

'Mary, you shouldn't twist your neck that way. You'll throw your back out of alignment.' Debra's awareness did not include what was actually happening, so Mary spelled it out.

'Debra, this is my job. Keep your voice down.'

'Oh, right. Anyway, I want to work on you again. I need to feel that place where you're coming from. It turns me on.'

Mary surrendered to the conversation. Debra's perfume proved smell was an equal fifth sense to the other four.

'I don't understand what you get out of it. You're the one who's doing all the work. I just lie there.'

'Oh no, massage is an exchange of energies. Your whole essence comes up into me through my hands. I pull you in.'

I can't argue with that, cookie, Mary thought to herself, as the vampire myths gained credibility. Debra's teeth seemed to grow a quarter of an inch as she fastened onto Mary's life force. And like Dracula before her, Debra was irresistible. There was too much flattery and too much beauty in the white, white skin showing through her body stocking for Mary to say no.

'Come Friday, seven o'clock, The Academy.'

'Yeah,' said Mary, imitating the whipped understatement of Joanne.

'The UPS truck is here,' called Martha from the back room.

'I've got to go. See you Friday.' Mary ran back to work.

Jimmy and Martha were pulling five boxes over the doorstep. Jimmy didn't break stride, but looked at her attentively, as he said 'Hi, Mary.'

His shoulders and back looked bigger than Mary remembered, more solid as Jimmy took up space in a comfortable, 'here I am' way. Men don't quiver like women do, she thought as she watched Jimmy. She wondered if she trembled like Heather and Debra. She could almost feel the blood flow through their veins when they put a hand on her arm. She suspected she did tremble, but always forced herself into a frozen posture hoping to look strong. Wherever she looked the only acceptable brand of strength was male imitation in both the straight and bent worlds. Mary was so angry at this distortion of her femininity. 'There are two sexes, not one,' she wailed inside, more volatile than usual. Jimmy was standing by with unmistakable intent.

'Hi, Jimmy,' she said exhausted by her own anger, too tired to hate him.

'Mary, there's a coffee shop in Venice with a jukebox and good pie. Would you go with me sometime? It's on me. I'm buying. Anything you want.' His body stood by like granite but his voice shook and jumped an octave as he said his speech all on one breath. Maybe Jimmy was faking it too, some tiny hopeful fantasy whispered to Mary.

'That might be OK. Thank you for inviting me.'

'Great. I think you'll like this place. It's cool.' He jumped in the truck, too amazed by her answer to formulate an actual plan. But that was fine for both of them. The possibility of a date was enough for that Monday.

At the week's end, Mary hurt from work. Thousands of items for the infant and toddler had been processed. Her hands were tired from shooting the garment gun that slid the plastic price tag holder through a seam in the cloth. And the smile for the customer was wearing thin, as Martha and Mary counted out the drawer at five o'clock on Friday. It was a perfectly run store and they numbered the cash, cheques, and credit card receipts down to the penny.

In theory, Mary looked forward to the massage as she showered and shaved her legs for Debra, but when she drove over Sepulveda into the setting sun, she braced herself for the encounter. The mandatory halter top, no bra and short shorts set off the gold cluster earrings that brushed Debra's shoulders. Had she been starring in a mini series about Estée Lauder, Debra's make-up could not have been more precise. Mary ordered her body into passivity as she wrapped herself in a large bath towel brought from home. Paul said 'hi' looking a little weaker than before.

'Still eating peas, Paul?'

'Oh yes, Mary, I'm so toxin-free, I'm beginning to see people's auras.'

'Really, what colour am I?'

'You're pure gold, Mary. Radiant.' Maybe this Paul guy deserved some reevaluation. Mary didn't know everything under the sun.

'What colour is Debra?'

'Same as you. Everybody's giving off gold light. It just took me a while to see it.'

'Oh, I'm not special?'

'God, yes, everybody's special, Mary.'

'No, I meant in the colour sense. I thought auras were blue, green, orange, purple, a whole rainbow.'

'So far all I'm seeing is gold, white light on everybody, except for this one bus driver the other day. He was a black hole. He took in light.'

'Maybe he was the devil's apprentice.'

'Oh, Mary, do you think so?'

Paul's literal belief system tolerated no whimsy. But he obviously liked her, so she let him go. She was just killing time before that first slap of Debra's hands on her shoulders. Lying on the gurney, eyes closed, Mary smelled Debra coming. Her perfume wasn't kidding around. Neither were her hands and her voice as she told Mary, 'Relax, darling, that's it. Let it go. What's that knot in your back? Oh, baby, that's some load you're carrying around. Give it to me. I'll take it. Mary, ease up.'

Mary heard something behind the breasts and the perfume and the make-up. Debra said her name from some deep spot that knew about despair and confusion. Did she know how long a girl could cry when the father wasn't there, when the male was so shadowy, the girl had to find it in herself to stop the shaking? Love came through Debra's hands. She cherished the hard knots on Mary's back as if they were her own, and Mary saw that place where she could fly, and someone would catch her.

'That's it. Mary. Go there. I'm with you. Let the back go. Yes, honey. That's it.' Debra's hands moved up the back to her neck, where she pulled on Mary's hair in little handfuls.

It was a startling moment. There was intuition and kindness beneath this child's manipulating ways, and Mary pretended to doze for a few minutes so no one would see her cry. When she opened her eyes, Debra was lying naked on another table letting Paul massage her feet. Mary tensed up again, thinking it was so unfair of her to flaunt her nakedness in front of this man, bent over in concentration trying to hide his hard-on. Mary's lust was taboo, but Paul's straightforward little arousal was a fair response to Debra's nudity, and Mary knew Debra was playing again.

'I can't stand them.' Debra told her in the changing room speaking of men. 'I hate intercourse, that endless pounding. It makes me so angry when I hear the neighbours downstairs humping away.'

Mary listened delicately never having harboured such sexual antagonism. Intercourse was the one good point she could see in the opposite sex, the one variable that offered some fun and respite from the daily chores. The bed held a connection for her, a common ground, the possibility of reconciliation, despite her current status. Debra's distilled femininity, purer and more demanding than a rock video, hid her hatred, and Mary was surprised by it.

'I guess that's why I identify with gay women. I don't want to be one, but I sympathise with them.' Mary gave up hoping to segue Debra's hatred of men into a very personal love for her. Instead she drove home, leaving Paul panting over Debra's feet. She wanted to tell him to give it up, but reasoned maybe he liked it.

Saturday morning, the spiritual bonding with Debra metamorphosed down a few notches into a really tough physical lust. Mary pulled on the sweat pants and ran up and down the hills of Hollywood, trying to contain the one and only thought in her head. Who could she call? Who could she transfer some of this energy onto?

There was one. There was one who would sleep with her without question, without romance, without having to get to know her. Lawrence, the pest.

'Lawrence, it's Mary.' She stood by the phone sweating from the run. 'Is *Rocky V* still playing?'

'Mary. Mary from the kiddy store. Of course, don't even ask. I've got the paper right here. Let's see, 2.30, 5.00, 7.30. You tell me.'

'2.30 too soon?'

'No. No problem. Wear a skirt and no underwear. Just kidding, just kidding. We'll eat and talk after.' Mary liked the first suggestion better, but kept her mouth shut. Lawrence didn't need any encouragement. Mary hadn't dressed for a man in a long time, and already resented it as she lined her green eyes with grey pencil. She settled on bluejeans and a black sweater, compromising with a red lipstick, which in her opinion made her look flashy.

'Mary, lipstick, well, well,' were Lawrence's first words when they met in front of the movie theatre in Westwood. Mary had her seven dollars in hand, when Lawrence added, 'Put it away, don't be silly.

Anyway, it's a matinee. It's only four. What do you get paid in retail, $7.50 an hour, so it's on me. What's the difference? One movie. Big deal.'

They didn't know it, but the negotiations had begun.

· *Eleven* ·

'So remember the chase scenes in *Smokey And The Bandit*. That was my lens.' By his lens, Lawrence meant he rented lenses and cameras to movie production companies. 'It's a small business. I don't get the big pictures, but I get enough. The production managers like me. I keep up. I go to Japan and Germany once a year. It's a state of the art thing. The Japs, Jesus, you can't keep up with them. Everyday they got a new camera. Did you see this new one, the one you throw away? They don't throw away nothing in their own country. You toss a cigarette butt in the street. Somebody picks it up and turns it into a T.V. or something.

'I've been all over. Thailand, Australia. I zoom in there with a lens faster than the other guys. You know these movies shooting in the jungle, something breaks down, they call me. I'm fast. I don't fuck around. I mean I don't do *Star Wars*, but there's hundreds of little pictures, Kung Fu crap, porno, action garbage.'

Lawrence loved his subject. Mary thought maybe sex was his excuse to get someone to come to his apartment and talk about movies. She could tell from his place, he liked living alone. It wasn't some dump to sleep in. He owned and obviously used a vacuum cleaner, and his kitchen was immaculate with nice dishes. The tough talk hid some sensitivity for soft clean sheets and bright primary-coloured bath towels. Neither of them were coy as they walked to his apartment after dinner. They both knew why Mary called.

'You need a plough-job, huh, kid. Yeah, I know, working in that kiddy store, I mean, after a while, you need some action. I know.' Lawrence didn't weigh much more than Mary. He was perfectly proportioned, but small. And hard everywhere, hard little head, hard nose, hard teeth. He didn't kiss her as he ploughed away without too much finesse, but one of his hands gently held her head throughout, which was nice. His scream was high, as he let go for a few quick seconds.

'Superb,' he said, pulling out right away, and Mary wasn't disappointed either, but wished he'd lingered just a moment longer. But he was up trotting around the room looking for a lens catalogue to show her. 'See, this is the retina filter Hitchcock used in *Rear Window*. It was a one time thing, never used before or since. What a picture, *Rear Window*, a classic.'

Mary dressed. She liked Lawrence because she didn't have to talk. It was just sex, it wasn't a big deal.

'So, now you know where I am, I'm here. Not that this is it. This dump, are you kidding. I've got my eyes on a condo. It'll kill you. Not this crappy wallpaper. Hand-picked stuff by a decorator. You'll see.'

'OK, Lawrence, thank you for the movie and everything. I'd better go. It's getting late.'

'Yeah, kid, drive safe.'

After the date with Lawrence, Mary retreated to her store and the non-sexual company of Raymond. The sun was rising in the desert sky over Los Angeles, as summer kicked in hot. While everyone complained about the soaring temperatures, Mary and Raymond revelled in it.

'Braised salmon with shallots and capers. What do you think?' Raymond asked her leafing through the latest copy of *Gourmet Magazine*.

'What's braised?'

'It's between steamed and sauteed. You keep a lid on the pan.'

'Sounds great.'

'We'll get salmon from Chalet Gourmet. It'll be about ten dollars a pound. Do we have enough money?'

'Sure, Lawrence paid for the movie. I've got seven extra dollars, and your sister sent you that twenty for your birthday, remember. You put it in the coffee tin.'

'Oh yes, what's happening to me? I can't re-member anything.'

'You're just not concentrating. You've got too much on your mind.'

Another purple bruise the size of a dime had appeared on Raymond's cheek. The cancer underneath pushed against his jaw distorting the shape of his face. He was a vain man, and this disfigurement did more to lower his morale than any actual symptoms. He sat in the car while Mary did his banking, but regained his old enthusiasm when they pulled into the parking lot of Chalet Gourmet, a ridiculously over-priced store that sold some of the freshest meat and fish in the city.

'Mary, I love you more than life itself, but I'm picking out the salmon. How do I look?'

'Gorgeous.' Back in the apartment, Mary rubbed a little makeup concealer over the cancer, and threw some bronzer on his cheekbones for colour.

'You look like Nancy Sinatra, it's uncanny.' Mary told him hoping to score a laugh.

'I was thinking more Marisa Berenson.' Raymond added, smiling a little. When Mary told Raymond about Lawrence, she could have been talking about changes in the weather. Sexual variety was not a concept that troubled Raymond.

'You know me, I stick to the boys, but it's a cowboy one week and a librarian the next. I just hope he's nice to you, and he pays, darling, which is not a bad quality. I couldn't believe you threw away all that money on that Heather.'

'You didn't like Heather?'

'She made eyes at me, for God's sake. When she was with you. What a pain. She was all over the place. Who am I to talk? Remember when I took that Greg to Hawaii. Hawaii, $3,000 later and I end up in the emergency ward when he stabbed me. Stabbed me, for God's sake. A nine inch scar for a three inch cock.'

At work Mary tried to pump life into the air conditioner by cleaning the filter and wiping the winter's soot off the vents. Martha joined her in dusting the top shelves of the store, refreshing the little unsold bears and lambs with a good shake, when the phone rang.

'Where you been, kid?' Lawrence spoke knowing his voice needed no introduction.

'I'm working, Lawrence, I'm at work.'

'I know, but I keep getting that damn machine of yours, so I thought I'd give you a holler. I'm hornier than a bull here.'

'Well, you're just going to have to hold it. I'm not in the mood.' She knew she could be straight with him, even though it wouldn't slow him down any.

'I'm sitting here pulling on it, Mary. I need you to give it a good jerk.'

'I'm at the store, Lawrence, stop it.' Without Debra to fan the coals, Mary couldn't work up a repeat performance with Lawrence, the pest. 'Please, don't call me here. I'm not available for a regular thing.'

Mary knew she was abrupt, but felt it was better than making some bullshit promise she might not be able to keep.

'I'm flying to Tokyo tomorrow for eight weeks.

I just wanted to slip it to you before I go.'
Mary understood that this was Lawrence's idea
of thoughtfulness, as ridiculous and selfish as it
appeared to be. He thought her horniness was
exactly like his and didn't want her going eight
weeks without a plough-job.

'Have a good trip, Lawrence, I hope you make
some money.'

'Money, that's easy. You girls, now that's a
problem. I'll call you when I'm back.'

He was cute, there was no getting around it, but
his buzzing gave her a headache and she was glad he
was leaving the country. Mary wondered if Debra
and Lawrence were on the same sexual timetable
when moments later, Debra sashayed into the store
dressed in pink. Pink on pink on pink as every
mother's head turned to look at this neon sign of
femininity. A pink blazer, whose length hit exactly
where her thigh met her torso, covered the sheerest
baby pink tights and a pink blouse with Hamlet
ruffles showing deep cleavage to just above the
navel. Another pair of Robin Hood boots, also pink,
completed the costume. Debra didn't carry a purse
which kept the look sleek, like she'd just stepped off
a cloud.

'Hi, Mary.'

'Martha, do we have any aspirin?'

'Yes, in the back. How many do you need?'

'Four. Hi, Debra.' Mary's low pressure, low
visibility job was leaving her too vulnerable a mark
for these drop-in visits. But it would be hard for
Mary to disappear any more deeply into the world

short of going to the Orient where she could run into Lawrence.

'Can you come this Friday?' Mary didn't think she was strong enough for another massage. With Lawrence out of the country, there was no release valve available, and Mary knew Debra was getting off on the tease.

'Listen, Debra . . . Martha, do you mind if I walk around the block? I've got to get some air for this head. Come on, Deb.'

'Sure, honey, get me some gum, okay.'

Mary spoke the minute they were out the door. 'Debra, stop it.' Too much stimulation and not enough release gave Mary a focus undissipated by the pink adornments. Instead of cutting off her hair, she cut off Debra. 'I'm in a constant state of arousal around you. I think you know it and I think you feed it. Get a boyfriend or a girlfriend, but stop playing me like a fish. I slept with a man the other day, for Christ's sake.'

'How was it?'

'I liked it.'

'I hate intercourse,' reminded Debra. A thin summer breeze stirred the ruffles around Debra's neck and her hair blew into her mouth. She brushed it aside with a manicured finger. Mary felt herself being pulled into a discussion about sex, and resisted the tug. 'The store is off limits. It's not a single's bar, it's for babies and mothers. Do you understand?'

'OK.' Debra watched all the men on the street watch her as she bent over to pick some microscopic lint off her boot. Her immediate transference of attention from Mary to every guy on the block, quelled any reservations Mary might have had about being too harsh.

'Good, I have to go back now.' And Mary ran fast to the drug store to get Martha's gum. She was holding a glass of water and the four aspirin, when Mary rejoined her in the back room, and they finished out the day tagging forty slumber sacs and one hundred ruffled rubber panties.

When she got home, Mary's phone machine registered Lawrence's four hang-ups and she decided then and there to do more than unplug the phone. She unplugged the machine. She didn't even want messages. Her hair was growing in and she needed quiet so this could happen. Other people needed quiet to think, and read, and sleep. Mary needed quiet to grow her hair. Too much noise and off it would come. With Lawrence and Debra out of the picture, Mary felt only relief, as she listened to the neighbours through the open summer windows. Their mattress hit the wall over and over as they moaned with pleasure.

Coming down hard on Lawrence and Debra accomplished exactly what Mary wanted. Days of nothing. It was difficult getting a woman to sleep with you, and Mary was tired. Plus Lawrence's male energy was too insistent for her to take for any long period of time.

Debra and Lawrence were the real couple. Without one Mary wouldn't have had the other. Lust for

Debra drove her into the arms of Lawrence. She doubted this would ever change. It was a circuitous route, and Mary needed to look at the map for a while before pressing on.

During the day she listened to Martha's stories about the ladies at church, like soothing fairy tales told over and over before bed. At night she babysat. Mrs Daladier told her to concentrate on the youngest. 'The other boys take care of each other, don't worry about them.' Little Arthur understood that his mother was leaving, and sobbed for his very life as the station wagon pulled out of the driveway. It was a tragic, desperate drama as he wailed, 'Mama, mommy, I want my mommy. Go away, I want mommy.' He trotted down the yard and threw his body on the fence as if he would perish from her absence. The older boys, somewhat indifferent but not completely hardened, told Mary they used to feel that way, but they didn't cry anymore. 'She's coming back, Arthur,' they yelled to the inconsolable toddler. Mary got every ball she could find, and showed them to Arthur. He pushed her away with renewed sorrow, until she showed him a pink and green foam rubber football. This was interesting. 'Football,' said Arthur between sobs. Mary bounced it off her head, her foot, her elbow, and finally her stomach. This killed Arthur. 'More,' he said as Mary bounced it off her stomach maybe twenty times. 'More.' Mary bounced the ball until it got too dark, and little Arthur took her hand and they went inside.

Mary found herself in the middle of the healthiest

family since the Swiss Robinsons. Television couldn't have invented this group, except maybe on Sunday at the tryouts for the American Olympic swim team. And they thought Mary was the coolest. She played basketball and baseball and didn't mind touching their pet snake.

The baby Arthur fell in love. 'Mary' he would scream, pulling at himself with excitement that didn't know what it was. Mrs Daladier winked and told Mary, 'Look, you're Arthur's first love.' There was not a moment when Mrs Daladier wasn't yelling at her boys, but they worshipped her. As much as they wanted Nintendo, they all laughed when they told Mary how their mother threw the VCR out the window.

'One morning, she just chucked it. And it's heavy, Mary.'

'The children were turning into robots.' Mrs Daladier said mildly, as she flung hamburger patties into sandwich bags to freeze for later. She belonged on the prow of a ship.

Work was quiet and steady except for the deliberate check-in calls from Jasmine. Mary could hear the sexy buzz of a movie set in the background.

'Hi, Mary, do you have a polka dot sleeper? I need a shower gift for an unborn baby. By the way, you're my best friend, you know.' Apropos of nothing.

'Well, good. Yes, we have sleepers in a variety of polka dots and just red and green if it's a Christmas baby.' Jasmine always liked detail, so Mary threw her some to let her know she'd heard.

'Nobody could ever replace you. You realise that, don't you?' Now who could Jasmine be talking about? The name never came up, as it filled the marquee in great big theatrical lights.

'Why don't you come over for dinner. Peter's in town and he'd love to see you.' I bet he would, thought Mary realising how chaste and respectful she was of both Peter and Jasmine in the hot little stew of Hollywood.

They never put a date on the invitation, but one can't underestimate the importance of a gesture. Maintenance calls kept the doors open, while Liz Tate fulfilled Joanne's prediction and disappeared into public life. When she made the cover of *People* magazine for marrying a convict, Brad Tillis, who was serving twenty years to life for armed robbery, the girls never mentioned it, but strained to keep from smiling. If they wanted to screw up their friendship they could have done worse. Ms Tate knew how to make her dreams come true. She was rehabilitating Brad Tillis with love letters and meetings with the Governor to review the penal system in America.

'Rehabilitate this,' Mary thought to herself, pointing to her crotch as she read how Liz fought for conjugal visits and lost, deferring to the state and the ferocity of the other inmates. Brad Tillis was a pussycat, but she didn't want to start a riot, *People* magazine explained. One might not be able to keep facts from the press, but one could still hide motives.

Mary decided then and there to approach life a little less poetically. Everything wasn't a metaphor. Sometimes people said exactly what they meant.

· *Twelve* ·

Mary's first date with Jimmy was a throwback. He tried to be the kind of guy she tried to be with Heather. He was responsible, attentive, heavy on opening doors and bill-paying. It wasn't so bad.

He added his own dimension as well. Jimmy was boring. But after Debra and Lawrence's high wire act, Mary was relieved to be bored. The pressure was off. They talked about cars for the first hour. Cars and later, buildings. These were Jimmy's best subjects.

'Fasten your seat belt, honey,' Jimmy reminded her as she climbed into the cab of his clean white pickup truck. He called her 'honey' so naturally and easily that it seemed exactly right. Jimmy was ready to take care of her for the evening. She knew he'd washed and filled the car, just as she had done for her dates with girls.

A deodorizer in the shape of a Christmas tree hung from the rear view mirror filling the compartment with heavy sweet fumes called 'pine tree forest' and a weighted bean bag anchored a coffee cup holder to the gear box. The rest was clean and shiny; Jimmy's home.

'I'm sorry the seats are so hard, but trucks don't come with plush interiors. I'm thinking of putting carpeting down. What do you think, Mary?'

It was a date. He was driving. Mary applied herself to the problem. 'What colour?'

'Blue.' He answered right away. 'But I may trade this in for a jeep. I really want four-wheel drive. You have so much more control.'

Driving was Jimmy's business, and the ride to the diner was in a class by itself. He drove in one smooth motion, anticipating problems blocks ahead. He didn't rush, but he didn't hesitate either as he clearly set the pace for the rest of the traffic. His truck didn't need soft seats. His eyes watched for every bump and pothole as he manoeuvred to the smoother parts of the road. If Jimmy had driven a Rolls Royce, he might have flown. As it was, his hard little truck felt like a limo when his hands took the wheel.

'What kind of a car do you have, Mary?'

'Nothing special. A Toyota.'

'They're good. I bet it doesn't break down on you.'

'Just once.'

'Those Japanese cars are well made, but I re-member the old Fords from 1969. The Mustang that year was one of the finest cars ever built. And it had pickup. The Japanese cars are good, but no real pep, except for the Lexus, and that's out of my range. I haven't driven a car with really good acceleration in years. Chevies had it. Eight miles to a gallon, but they drove like a son of a bitch. Excuse my French, Mary.'

Jimmy made her chaste, so she responded seriously, 'That's OK.'

'I was a maniac when I was a kid, Mary. See all these buildings. They weren't here twenty years ago. Me and my brothers, we'd hop into my dad's Chevy, and blast out Olympic Boulevard at eighty, ninety miles an hour, then cut down Lincoln to Redondo Beach. He wasn't my real dad. He was my foster dad. My real dad was alive, but he was a big alchy. Mom left him and us, and he dragged us around the bars. We slept in the car, until the courts gave us to my foster parents. It was great though, Mary. It wasn't like TV. We didn't see it that way. The bars were fun. Old guys taught us magic tricks. I must have lived on pretzels and coke. Dad didn't hit us or anything. He couldn't find his nose, poor guy. Just a big lush. My foster parents, they straightened me out. We went to church and summer camp. They taught me things, how to keep clean and neat, how to work. They gave me my own room. My foster Dad, he took me to Yosemite, showed me how to fish and hunt. I can live in the woods, Mary.'

Another stray. Joanne and now Jimmy, hiding out, telling Mary how great their lives were with these stories from hell.

'Here we are, Mary. Watch your step, there's some oil there by the curb.'

Mary, made dainty by this Jimmy, jumped over the sludge. It was a real diner with wide booths and a menu featuring shakes and malts, tuna melts and burgers, and fries with gravy; the whole thing transplanted from some Midwest town to become a California gold mine.

'Anything you want, Mary.' She ordered a hot turkey sandwich and milk.

'Good call. You get mashed potatoes with it and carrots. I'll have a double cheeseburger, large fries, and a chocolate malt. Whew, we made it.'

'Good driving, Jimmy.

'You know, it's funny. I like to drive after driving all day. Sometimes after work, I get my own car and drive around for two or three more hours. With the UPS truck I have to worry. It's their vehicle, I have a schedule to keep, but in my car, I just cruise. Mary, I know places in L.A. nobody knows about. Maybe I could show you after dinner.'

Mary's mind kept busy as she listened to Jimmy talk. He spoke in the same flat monotone as Joanne. The words themselves were the emotional content. No feeling allowed, as Mary wondered if the lack of consistent, singular parents created these voices with no colour, no commitment, and no conscious opinion about their lives.

It was like being with deaf people who spoke in high-pitched imitation never having heard how they were supposed to sound. Or watching blind people who didn't know that human beings stood still.

'Honey, be careful of your sleeve. There's some butter there by your elbow.'

'Oh, thanks. I hate getting dirty.'

'I know that about you. I'm the same way.' His voice rose for the first time that evening as he found something in common with Mary. Once again she liked sitting with a person who had absolutely no expectations of life.

Mary had been raised to be a success. In her own right, not just by marriage. She had been exposed to every cultural event and expensive classroom on the East coast, and could hold forth with exceptional poise on politics, religion, literature, philosophy, and the smaller fashionable sub-subjects like rock and roll and the movies. But it was the quiet of no expectation that held promise and discovery for her. The endless stream of information, high and low, which she unfortunately retained in entirety, eventually overwhelmed her into leaving it all behind.

It was Jimmy's lack of history that was so comforting. He was the most unstimulating man Mary had ever met, and finally she could hear herself think.

They just sat. Mary didn't know what Jimmy was watching, but she was watching his mouth. She was sure his front teeth were cheap caps. They were too perfect, square and protruding a little, wrong for his lip, in a way that nature is never wrong. He strained to get the lip over the teeth to sip his coffee, like a horse taking a piece of sugar.

'Mary have you ever seen the steepest street in L.A.?'

'No, I don't think so.'

'Great. This is going to be fun.' He picked up the bill, flipped his wallet out of his back pocket, lay down the money, and put a toothpick in his mouth. Mary thought it was a lot like being out with Joanne. It was getting dark, and she entered Jimmy's world as they fastened their seat-belts for the ride back to Silverlake and the city's steepest street. He didn't demand she pay attention, as he showed her the city through his eyes.

'Look at the streetlights, honey, they're just going on. Twilight triggers the system.' Mary looked up to see a brace of lamps quiver with green light for a moment before coming on full strength. Then a quarter of a mile down the road, another ten blocks of lights flickered and then glowed orange.

'The orange ones are newer. They really warm a street.' Jimmy's movie was pretty good. It didn't have people in it, but the scenery was something to see. Hard city scenery without filters to make it softer or better.

'Lock your door, Mary, this neighbourhood is rough.'

It wasn't that rough. Jimmy wanted it to be, so he would have a good story for Mary. They were many blocks north of the really dangerous streets, but Jimmy wanted to protect her and it wasn't an entirely unpleasant sensation. Even if it was a joke. Mary was an urban animal, bred for survival in Manhattan and New Jersey, but lordy, lordy, she tried to look fluttery as the big, bad trucks drove by.

'Look, there it is.' They climbed out of the flats into the far Eastern end of the Hollywood Hills known as Silverlake. It was a roller coaster thrill as he deliberately slowed the truck at the top of a hill before showing Mary the drop on the other side.

'I hope the truck can make it,' he said down-shifting dramatically, and over they went. Mary screamed and touched his arm, and Jimmy spoke to himself under his breath, 'Now this is fun.'

'Let's do it again.' Jimmy said, turning the truck around to climb back up the hill. They did it two more times, until Jimmy said he should probably give the gears a rest. 'I'll drive you home through the park.' As Jimmy and Mary drove past Dodger Stadium, deep into Griffith Park, it got country dark.

'Big park.' Mary whispered, as five low-rider Mexican cowboys cruised by in a purple car. 'Don't worry, you're safe as a baby. I'm an attack-trained UPS man. And the Police Academy is right up the road. They drill in these hills and everybody knows it.' Mary moved closer to Jimmy suspecting he'd planned it that way. She would have. A little fantasy fear always brought Heather closer. And fear of a python was the only thing that got Joanne within touching distance. It was a fair ploy and Mary let it work for a while, relieved she wasn't the one thinking up the manoeuvres. Jimmy pulled up in front of her apartment. He wanted to sit, but Mary's attempt at dating a man was hanging by a thread and she quickly escaped. The good-humoured tolerance for car talk and riding up and down hills had it's limits, and Mary knew she'd better respect them or lose what little patience she had.

Reassured by the safety of her apartment, Mary softened and wanted to explain her Cinderella disappearance. She gave Jimmy ten minutes to drive home, and called.

'Jimmy, hi, it's Mary. Listen, I know I rushed out on you, but there's a reason.'

'I understand, Mary. You don't even know me.'

'No, well, you're sweet, but that's not exactly it. You see, I've been dating girls for a couple of years.'

'My sister's gay. It's not a big deal. I still want to go out with you, Mary.'

He didn't miss a beat. Mary suspected Jimmy thought this was just another way for a girl to say 'no' to quick sex and he respected it, and ignored it. Mary was mildly touched as she found out how many men took her sexual announcement as a very minor deviation from the norm. Certainly nothing to stop their single-minded pursuit of consummation. Women were shocked, repelled, or attracted, but the men just continued to press doggedly toward the mark if they were interested in the first place.

'So, I don't know if I can do this, Jimmy.'

'Just take a walk with me next Friday. We'll get ice cream and rent a video.'

'I don't want you thinking we'll have sex or anything.'

'Can I put my arm around you?'
'No.'
'Can I hold your hand?'
'No.'
'Can we sit on my sofa together?'
'Maybe, if there's at least three feet between us.'
'Two feet?'
'No. By the way, is your sister cute?'
'Not as cute as me.'
'Bye.'
'Bye.'

· *Thirteen* ·

Raymond checked into the hospital for the first time. One of his eyes wasn't scanning, and they wanted to flush his system with massive doses of antibiotic. He called her the night before.

'Mary, one of my eyes isn't moving.'

'Can you see through it?'

'Yes, but it's frozen. I've called the doctor. He wants me at Hollywood Community tomorrow morning. Could you drive me?'

'Sure. No prob.' Mary, self-consciously casual, spoke as if it were nothing. In the morning, she took his hand and guided him to the elevator. Still Hercules from the neck down, his whole body trembled like an earthquake that doesn't stop.

'Try not to shake, Raymond.'

'I'm too scared.'

Mary started to cry and they both gave into it. They held hands and sobbed in the elevator, the garage, and finally, the car.

'I can't drive,' said Mary.

'I can't see,' said Raymond.

'Oh God. Remember when we first met and you lived in that apartment with the clouds painted on the walls? I thought you were a prince. I never knew someone could paint clouds on everything.'

'Everything. The walls, the ceiling, the floor. It was my cloud period. I loved you from the moment I saw you. I'd never seen a girl look at everything so carefully. You always tried to understand things. Me, I take everything for granted, but you notice things. You noticed me.'

'Well . . . a six foot hairy Italian with red glasses and a lot of attitude.'

'Too grand?'

'Not really. Grandiosity is all we have, if you'll notice.'

'Can you drive now, Mary?'

'Yeah.'

'Let's go.'

Raymond settled into his bed on the AIDS floor of Hollywood Community. His nurse, Pauline, should have been in show business, but wasn't wasting her talent, as she shot one-liners to her boys.

'Try not to get too hot for me, angel,' she told Raymond's roommate as she rubbed his back. Her life force charged the rooms with energy and everyone borrowed some as they struggled to stay alive.

'Pauline, darling, I need you.'

'Put it back in your pants, sailor.'

It was corny as hell, but Pauline tried so hard, it was impossible not to laugh. Raymond and Mary looked at Pauline like the saviour she was.

'Okay, children, autographs later. Get into bed, Ray. Give me that arm. Wow, get back Arnold, now that's a muscle. Be still, my heart. Mary, pussycat, I have to do some nasty things to this boy.'

'I'll be okay, Mary. I'll call you later.'

'Hang in there, Raymond. See you, Pauline.'

Mary made it to the hospital lobby before she realised she'd forgotten her car keys. A momentary panic drove her to the elevator fast and she burst into Raymond's room without knocking. There was blood on the walls and the sheets were soaked red as Pauline and another nurse tried to insert a piccline deep into Raymond's spurting vein. He held his other bloody arm above his head to stop the flow from failed first attempts; every wound a potential site for infection within hours. He saw Mary with the one eye that was tracking, and his look of unspeakable horror drove her backwards into the bathroom, where she grabbed the handrail and threw up.

· *Fourteen* ·

Mary knew Jimmy put the world together in the simplest, cleanest terms because that was all he could tolerate. 'Mary, if I get angry, I'll punch someone to death. When I was a kid, I threw a few barflys through plate glass. They sent me to jail and I deserved it. But those guys deserved it too. That's why I'm always telling you, don't walk around alone at night. There are crazy people out there, Mary.'

There were many bogey men in Jimmy's world. Haunted houses in L.A. was another favourite theme. He clipped articles from the newspaper confirming his superstitions. With it's darker history to exploit, Hollywood was a perfect neighbourhood for Jimmy. He paid attention when Mary told him she was going to housesit for the Daladiers, and their house was probably haunted. She made this discovery when Mrs Daladier, after explaining the dog food and plant care, lowered her voice for confidentiality and said there was one other thing.

'Mary, you know me. I'm not crazy. I'm on the school board. I'm raising four children. We barbecue. But I think I should warn you. There's a ghost in the house. I just wanted to tell you because if you see it, you won't be scared. It won't hurt you, but sometimes it does throw things. It threw a spool of thread at me in my sewing alcove.'

'What does it look like?' Mary played the game because she adored Mrs Daladier and it was something to do.

'It's a woman. She's dressed in a long white gown. I've seen her in the dining room and little Arthur saw her out by the pool.' Mary wondered why ghosts always dressed in white. How come a ghost never wore a tank top and cut-offs? She kept her observations to herself and joined in the drama with a gasp and widened alert eyes, but she was not scared.

'Little Arthur saw the ghost?'

'Yes, and he had no prior knowledge.' Except every cartoon on TV, four solid Halloweens, and three brothers who tormented him constantly. Mary contained her doubts as Mrs Daladier continued.

'Sometimes children see the truth, Mary.' They nodded significantly and Mary took the keys to the house.

Mrs Daladier resumed her normal tone of voice. 'If you want to bring a friend and barbecue, there are ribs in the freezer. Help yourself. We love you, darling. We couldn't go on this vacation if it weren't for you.' Then Mrs Daladier hugged her and kissed her on the cheek. It was the hard, nurturing stamp of approval kiss of a natural mother. There was no sex in it. It was fierce like an injection, then soothing like the rush of the sedative after the injection; a kiss that bestowed strength and confidence and a woman's love for a woman, without apology. Mary stood up a little straighter, as she guarded Mr and Mrs Daladier's house.

She spent the first night in the master bedroom looking for the ghost. With four children, the house was a barely controlled explosion. The living room remained formal while the den overflowed with crayons and science projects, some deliberate and some, forgotten as old gummi bears, gathered lint in the corners. Mary relaxed her vigil with the pleasure of family chaos all around her. Two huge dogs protected her from real predators and her cynicism protected her from ghosts.

Mary decided to be nice to Jimmy, grudgingly, and without a hint of flirtatiousness, but still nice.

'You can come for a swim on Sunday, if you want to. I have this house and everything. Maybe we'll see the ghost.' He showed up at exactly 2.00 by the digital clock, as they had decided. Mary pointed out the land marks: a lemon tree, an orange tree, the vegetable garden, and finally an avocado tree.

'There aren't any avocados, though.' Mary had hunted, hoping to find a single, overlooked fruit for her dinner.

'Sure there are,' said Jimmy as he pointed out one after another, camouflaged green on green, invisible to Mary's city eyes.

The pool area held a lot of possibility for both of them. They might see the ghost, and they would definitely see each other. Jimmy was white except for his lower arms and neck, a UPS tan. Mary knew he couldn't stop watching her as she rode the mattress float into the middle of the pool. He sat on a deck chair staring at her body. Since he knew she liked girls, she didn't have to hide behind playboy femininity, and rode the float like a boy, open legged, finding a position for comfort rather than presentation. It turned her on, and Jimmy sat hypnotized on his chair, as she watched the reflected pool light fill his hazel eyes with life.

The August sun tanned them in half an hour, more than enough time for Jimmy to poke up through his trunks. Mary kept the float at a distance, enjoying her exhibitionism, and the effect it was having on Jimmy. She imagined what it was like to be Jimmy watching her settle into the sun and water. She wished she could make love to herself. Ten minutes into this fantasy, Mary said, 'Maybe the ghost is in the house. Want to look?'

Jimmy stood up, and Mary stirred the water propelling the raft to the pool's edge. She dawdled, stopping for a drink in the kitchen. Jimmy stood by like a cadet waiting for orders, while Mary wondered where they could do it. The Terminator-covered walls in the older boys' bedrooms weren't right, and Arthur's room was still a nursery. Mary knew what she knew all along. Jimmy took her hand and she led him to the most inviting spot in the house, maybe the whole neighbourhood; the marriage bed of Mr and Mrs George Daladier.

The kissing wasn't good. Jimmy's mouth hadn't adjusted to the bad caps, and Mary quickly turned her head to avoid the lips and teeth that didn't work together. Jimmy's huge chest, still hot from the sun, warmed her. That was okay, and she allowed her mind to drift back to herself on the float, legs apart, deliberately watching the sun through the eucalyptus trees to burn out the images of Heather and her twenty-four hour a day seduction. Heather, who put her hand low on Mary's waist when Mary signed her Visa bill in a crowded restaurant. Heather who kissed her for hours during bad rented movies on the VCR. That was the difference. With Heather it was all foreplay. With Jimmy, it was pretty much the main event. She slipped back into fantasy.

Mary threw herself on herself on the raft in the shallow end. Both Marys kept their eyes open, hiding nothing from each other as they admitted to lusting from their kneecaps to their elbows. The hard bony places with no nerve endings felt like a million, as the real sex spots came out from hiding, the slightest attention focusing all of life into a centimetre of skin. And through it all, Mary watched the sun from both sides. On her back she watched it direct in the sky. On her stomach she followed it filtering through the pool water, the diamond patterns reflecting off the trees as she flipped over again. Jimmy penetrated and Mary closed her eyes and gasped. He was quiet, a quiet boy, taking his sex as a tiny joy given to him if he was very good, and no one was looking.

'Mary, I think I see the ghost,' he said with closed eyes.

'She's beautiful. I can see through her white dress. She's smiling at me.'

'I see her too,' Mary said, only the ghost she saw was wearing a tank top and cut-offs and eating an avocado.

Jimmy wanted to linger, tired from his efforts. Mary tried to be still and enjoy the afterglow that movies told her was so important. But no luck, she had to move. She told Jimmy to sleep and ran down to the pool, swimming a fast twenty laps. The separation felt as good as the sex.

· *Fifteen* ·

Jimmy was a nice sweet choice for seduction. Never doubting his violent nature for a second, Mary knew he would kill himself first before hurting a woman. Mary more than admired his code of honour, she needed it. It protected her when she got angry at him. And eventually she would get angry, and Jimmy would let her pound it out.

'Idiot, moron, crazy drivers. Do you know what it's like to be a single woman in Hollywood?' Mary's first words as she entered Jimmy's apartment on their second date.

'Honey, I've told you not to drive on Hollywood Boulevard on Saturday night. I wouldn't, and I'm a big guy. Why didn't you let me pick you up?'

'Sure, and become your prisoner for the evening. And please, I can't stand your fucking paranoia. Everybody's a criminal to you. Just because you're a criminal doesn't mean everybody else is. God, I hate you.'

'Honey, I know. The traffic drives me crazy too.'

'It's not the goddamn traffic. Everything's so simple to you.' Jimmy had just impressed the hell out of Mary with his easy empathetic answer for her fury. But she wasn't done.

'It stinks in here. What's that smell? Why do you sleep in the living room? It's disgusting. I don't know what I'm even doing here. Now I suppose we have to have sex again just because we did it last time. I don't want to. Can I just sit and relax or are you going to bug me to death?'

'Honey, I think you're scared.'

'Oh, when did you get your degree in therapy? That's another thing I hate. How do you know what I'm feeling? This apartment is a pit. It totally turns me off. Zero sex appeal. You too. I want to go home. I never want to see you again.'

'That's pretty strong language, honey.' Her bomb was almost diffused with that one. Part of Mary stood back stunned at his patience. 'Pretty strong language' was a mild, neutral response. She tried to hold onto the hatred, but slow Jimmy showed her that her madness wasn't a fiendish, isolating demon, but bad traffic and a nasty city street and fear.

'I'm just like you, Mary. Only I don't have the words to say it. I go red and end up in jail.' Why did this jailbird have to get smart on her?

'I'm leaving,' Mary said with no resolve in her voice.

'I bought that tea you like, and I rented *The Bad Seed*. Have you ever seen it?'

'*The Bad Seed*. Like me. You wanted me to watch myself?'

'No, I just love this movie. I would have watched it alone if you hadn't come over. It's great.'

'But just a movie, no sex.'

'Honey, we'll take a walk on Melrose later if you want.'

Mary sat down, exhausted by her rage. 'Can you turn the fan off, please? It's so loud.' The fight was over and forgotten for Jimmy as he turned the fan off and started the movie.

Like Jimmy, his apartment demanded nothing. There were no pictures to admire, no collections to rave over, no cooking to praise, no important work to discuss. He owned only the possessions essential for survival. This eliminated choice and it's complexities. There were three places to sit, one place to sleep, and one of each of life's tools. Mary knew Jimmy would have preferred to own one fork, one knife, one spoon and one plate, but kept a few extra utensils to remain social in the world.

Tonight he had a date so he stocked up. Apart from the special tea for Mary, the contents of his refrigerator were stunning in their nutritional retardation. A loaf of Wonder bread, peanut butter and jelly, and a fresh package of bologna sat on the second shelf. One quart of whole milk, French's mustard and Kraft mayonnaise lined the condiment rack, and a new package of hot dogs completed the selection in case they wanted a hot meal.

'I know I don't eat right, Mary. Everybody tells me, but this is what my real Dad gave us, and look at me.' Point one for Jimmy. 'And be honest, Mary, doesn't that stuff look delicious?' Point two. Mary hadn't eaten white bread in ten years, so one Saturday night wasn't going to kill her, as she used Jimmy's other knife to spread mustard, mayo, and bologna on two identical slices of white, white bread.

They sat deep in the formless cushions of the sofa-bed eating their sandwiches.

'Why do you sleep in the living room?' Mary asked when she saw the one bedroom sitting empty next to the military bathroom. Again, one bar of soap, one toothbrush, one comb, one shaving kit lined up in order of use.

'I get lonely in the bedroom. I've never slept in a bedroom in my life. It doesn't feel right.'

Mary envied the closet which Jimmy showed her. It contained one suit, one tie (black leather – Jimmy wasn't without style) three white dress shirts, maybe ten casual T's and sweats folded precisely on a top shelf, three jeans; one blue, one stone washed and one black, and three pairs of shoes. Mary didn't love Jimmy, but she loved his shoes. Black dress shoes, high-top sneakers and black cowboy boots were it. Expensive and well-maintained, the three choices simplified decision making. In point of fact, rubber flip-flops in the bathroom made a fourth pair.

Jimmy and Mary had come to similar conclusions about owning things. Too much was too compli-cated. But Jimmy's minimalism was far deeper than

Mary's. He didn't know about pretty or the non-essential item. There was an element of true poverty in Jimmy's spareness. He made adequate money, but had no idea how to spend it. His life was pure function, starving for art and music. Only the movies showed him an alternative to the UPS route and the brown uniform.

They enjoyed each other's company, finding that solace that victims do when they are together and there are no oppressors around. Jimmy stayed true to his word, taking her on a walk rather than to bed. He held her hand the whole time like a young lover, and gave her a bad, toothy kiss by her car.

· *Sixteen* ·

Raymond stayed in the hospital for six weeks while they flushed his body with antibiotics. The doctors told him his vision would heal at the end of that time. It didn't. He saw clearly out of two eyes, but they pointed in different directions. He decided to use one eye on one day and one eye on the other, alternating with a black eye patch. Some rare brain virus, normally inhibited by a healthy immune system, was having its way in Raymond's head. He maintained his weight plus twenty-five pounds by eating five and six meals a day. The weight gave him power. If he was big he couldn't die. Mary brought him pizzas like they were cookies, and chocolate shakes boosted by supplements from the health food store. Eating became life, an affirmative statement of the will to fight.

'Do you have any powdered sugar?' Mary was reading from Gourmet Desserts.

'Why?'

'Almost every recipe in here calls for dusting with powdered sugar.'

'Dust this.' Raymond said pointing to his crotch. 'I've had it with these gourmet magazines. Let's get Bisquick, butter and milk, and dust hot dough balls with chocolate syrup and strawberry jam. And maybe a quart of ice cream. And bananas. And chocolate chips.'

Half an hour later, home from the store, they threw the lumpy balls of Bisquick onto a greased pan, and twenty minutes after that, ate enough sugar to boost the spirits of a third world country.

'Let's upholster the whole apartment.' It was Raymond's latest craze. They bought huge bolts of cotton padding, two staple guns and a striped fabric like Joseph's coat. Starting with Raymond's headboard, they moved along to the two end tables and finally upholstered the bookshelves lining the hall.

'Everything's going to be soft.' Raymond double padded the headboard.

'And colourful,' added Mary.

'Yep, I've had it with that muted shit. No more beige, grey, and black. No more mint green, no more Heather for Christ' sake. I want bright. I want jungle. Oh, Mary, that's a thought. Let's paint leaves on the ceiling.'

'How?'

'We'll get a leaf stencil, and spray them on. It's easy.' They bought leaf stencils and fruit stencils and vine stencils. Raymond was frantic to find banana stencils, but finally had to settle for a Chiquita poster of a bunch of bananas that could be cut out and then traced.

'I need yellow, Mary. It's a primary colour. I need it to set off the green and purple. Do you think monkeys would be too much?'

'Maybe just a touch too busy.'

They painted and ate. Raymond swallowed every pill, tincture, and homeophathic remedy along with the more traditional medication. Tea from Chinatown, herbs from Little Tokyo, mushrooms from Bulgaria, steroids from America, any rumoured boost for his fragile system. And he held. His T-cells stayed at 500, a reasonably hopeful figure for an HIV positive male.

'Mary, 500, I'm going to make it. There were guys alive on the AIDS ward with fifty. 500 for three months now. I think it's the ginseng. Or maybe the ice cream. I'm just going to keep on doing what I've been doing. It's working, Mary. Maybe they'll put me on the cover of *Time* magazine.'

'I think it's the paint fumes.' Mary jumped down from the ladder, a fine mist of green dusting her hair and face.

'It's water soluble. It'll wash right out. During my cloud period, I used an oil base. I had white hair for an entire winter. Santa Claus.'

Blood work was the new catch phrase. Eating and painting continued between blood work, the now monthly tests to determine Raymond's strength. There was a hiatus of almost six months where no symptoms appeared, and the apartment blossomed lush and tropical, and Mary's hair grew. Raymond burnt white sage, an Indian trick to purify the air of both germs and demons. Inevitability was the enemy. The new age visualized health, while the old age hunted for symptoms. Mary put his mind to rest many times when Raymond caught a cold, and Mary had one too.

'Raymond, it's January, everybody's got a cold. It's normal.'

'You too, are you sure, Mary?'

'I can't hear. I can't talk. I'm totally stuffed up. Don't worry.' But Mary's cold didn't turn into pneumonia and Raymond's did.

They put him in an oxygen tent and he lost twenty pounds. Pauline had gone blond for Raymond's second hospital stay.

'What do you think, Mary? Don't I look like Madonna now?' Pauline vogued into the room.

'Identical. Thank God you told me. I was about to ask for your autograph. How's Raymond?'

'Pretty good. He'll beat this pneumonia. His T's are still at 400. That's very strong. He just needs a lot of sleep so he can fight this off.' Pauline knew more about AIDS than the doctors. Driven by an awesome talent for love, she made friends with men who were dying. Mary brought her a gardenia for her new blond hair.

Raymond needed Pauline desperately, and so did Mary. If the AIDS ward hadn't been so tough, Mary would have stayed longer just to watch Pauline's terrible, sprayed, white blond hair never move as she kept five or six men alive. Pauline was the opposite of a vampire as she gave her overflowing extra blood to the thin, bruised men who had to count their few remaining red cells.

Mary's mental tirade started as she drove home, surrounded by promised death, hunting for a god, and realising her beloved, strengthening, all-powerful, spiritual Father had absolutely no female qualities whatsoever. Her rational head knew God was above gender identification, but her body and soul, mad with grief, wanted a god with a belly to crawl into.

Mary's feminism took a savage turn, when she wondered if conventional psychotherapy, the accepted, educated pill for depression, anger, and failure, was systematically teaching her generation to hate women. When all was said and done, wasn't it basically suggesting that mommy wasn't good enough? Mary remembered the time, pretty much throughout the sixties and seventies, when saying you liked your mother was a social gaffe comparable to calling a black person a nigger.

The worm was on the inside, disguised by expensive fees and understanding eyes, patiently explaining random anger at a salesperson or colleague or lover, by asking, 'Who do they remind you of?' And the patient or client pleases the doctor by dutifully answering, 'Mother'.

Then the doctor nods significantly, while poor mother back home in Minneapolis bakes a pie and takes the flack. Women, the majority of doctor's patients, were learning to hate women, as they tried to stay liberated with a subscription to *Ms* magazine and a hard-won coffee break pencilled into the contract on a slave job.

Mary rode the tiger in her head, unable to find a balance, but knowing there was truth in the extremity.

Eventually Mary prayed to a minor god she'd seen in a museum. The sacred figure had earrings and breasts and six arms to hold her. She imagined her new god dizzy with incense and pleasure, pomading her hair and chattering away about immortality. Mary finally slept.

· *Seventeen* ·

There were six more nights at Jimmy's over a six week period. In noticing Jimmy, the other sex made a comeback into Mary's field of vision. Jimmy was the bridge. Standing still for her fury, he pulled the other men into visibility, and she saw them standing for their bosses, standing for the pay cheques they must bring home. A mouth would catch her eye, or the soft underside of an upper arm twice the size of hers. But more than sexual characteristics, she noticed the grace under pressure. She didn't understand that it was there for her. It was the male statement of love.

Jimmy's apartment was the cave they crawled into together. It was a cave not by some poetical transformation in Mary's mind. It was a cave by the smell; something close to his bologna and hot dog diet, and by the light; none. Mary, angry to be on a date with a man on principle, allowed herself to be soothed down over a three hour period.

'Mary, I rented *The Egg And I* with Fred McMurray and Claudette Colbert.' His choice surprised her, until she noticed Jimmy owned only one book, a paperback encyclopedia of the movies. She leafed through it, standing, too nervous to sit down.

'Honey, look in the ice box. I bought a big box of Velveeta. And Winchell's donuts for later. Thirteen assorted for two dollars and fifty cents.'

'I don't eat donuts.'

'I think there's an orange in there.'

'What happened, you bought it by mistake?'

'There's a tree outside. I picked it for you.'

'Oh.'

Mary sat on the floor, not wanting to commit to the intimacy of the sofa. Jimmy, behind her, easily placed his two hands on her shoulders. There didn't seem to be a pass in the touch, as he spent most of the movie petting and rubbing her neck and arms.

'Honey, why don't you sit up here with me.' Something about the smell, and the flickering black and white images, and Claudette Colbert got Mary into a prone position on the couch, with Jimmy lying the length of his body behind her. There was little sensuality in the cuddling, and Mary settled into Jimmy's sleepy, uncomplicated, donut-sedated vibes. A Winchell's donut contact high, pleasant and dopey. She felt his penis thicken against her back like a big chunk of Velveeta. He didn't try to put it anywhere for at least an hour, but nibbled at her neck, like a walrus with its two long teeth on the outside.

Mary didn't mind when he turned her over as the credits rolled. Jimmy didn't have an erotic bone in his body as he took off his pants and asked her to do the same with one word, 'Honey.' But Jimmy's drawing card was safety and sweetness, as he entered her and eventually came quiet like the good boy he was. He fell asleep almost immediately on top of her, which Mary liked. She didn't have to talk. She let his weight iron out her thin, strained muscles, and finally sighed not in orgasm, but in funky comfort. They both slept through the night, unconsciously disengaging hours later.

The next five evenings were similar if not identical. On the fourth Saturday, he appeared agitated as he opened the apartment door.

'Mary, honey, I forgot the movie. Let's drive tonight.' She heard a note of urgency enter his emotional and vocal monotone.

'Okay.' Mary watched Jimmy drive as he took care of some disturbance in his psyche. His bad teeth ground against each other as he pointed out warehouse after warehouse downtown, dark and closed for the night. The buildings calmed him down.

Even the winos living on the edge of the neighbourhood didn't find their way into the vast flats alongside the railroad tracks to the rest of the country. The simplicity of the pattern was old and Western. Mary could easily imagine cattle and horses driven to this final American city, grazing next to the one storey buildings, altered only by electricity and refrigeration.

'I deliver here; cold storage for beef, and here; a novelty company. I deliver there; it's a sweatshop for plastic flowers. The Mexican women work there all day for two dollars an hour. I deliver there; transmission parts. That's my building; shoes. That one over there; candy. That one's my Friday route; paper goods. That's Wednesday, over there; first aid supplies. That black building; computer parts. How are you doing, Mary, OK?'

'Sure, Jimmy, I like seeing your route.'

'Yeah, my route. Mary, I hit a statuary today. I was delivering fountain parts, and the right back end of my truck nicked this Cupid thing holding grapes. It's $250 out of my paycheck. The guy was pretty mellow. He said it's between me and him. UPS won't know.'

'I'm sure he means it.'

'You think so, honey? I'm so glad you said that. I don't want to get fired.' Jimmy would have cried if he didn't have his gears to shift and buildings to inventory.

'That's mine, over there; baseball hats. Next to it; trash bags.' Mary wished they were riding in an old-fashioned car with a continuous front seat. She wanted to sit closer to Jimmy, but the modern, belted, impact-bagged, separated seats protected them from everything including intimacy. She did with words what she wanted to do with her body.

'Is your truck OK?'

'Fine, good as new. That statuary stuff crumbles if you just touch it, Mary. I'm a good driver. It's what I do. Twenty years with no tickets. I've got the lowest insurance rates in the city. If they fire me, I'm dead.'

'Jimmy, they won't fire you. They won't even find out. You'll pay the guy. People understand more than you think. He's probably making a profit anyway. That Cupid might have cost him 150 bucks.'

'No, he told me he's charging me the wholesale price.'

'Well, there you go. It's nothing to him. It's not a big deal.'

'You're positive, Mary?'

'I'd bet money on it.'

Jimmy took a breath. 'Have you ever seen the entrance to the subway they never built?'

'No.'

'Let's go. It's cool.'

They drove to an unlit, vacant lot behind Chinatown. Museum-worthy graffiti painted the stone arch over the tunnel entrance that went nowhere. A chain link fence torn from its hinges rested against the opening blasted into the base of a hill.

'I don't want to go any closer. Between the gangs and the homeless, it's pretty dangerous here,' Jimmy whispered and Mary, who didn't need urban drama as much as Jimmy, saw that it was a place to be killed.

'Even the mentals know enough not to go into the tunnel. Only the big, mean guys with guns sleep in there.' Mary saw Jimmy was back to himself, his eyes shining with city stories to impress her.

They looked at the L.A. skyline, backdropping this pit from hell and the rinky-dink Chinese dragons and Mandarin roofs of Chinatown. It was their city, pretending to be all cities for TV and movies, with its New York blocks, Boston blocks, London blocks, Paris blocks, Hong Kong blocks, small town blocks and suburban blocks. Growing without boundaries into the desert like the *Star Wars* grid, the city absorbed people from all over the world to fight, make up and change into the Americans they'd seen in the movies. The century was turning, and Jimmy and Mary hoped the angels were guarding the millenium.

On the sixth Saturday, Jimmy asked Mary if she loved him. With the first breath before the first word of the first equivocating phrase, Jimmy and Mary knew she didn't. It meant they wouldn't go on.

The neatness of the package surprised them both. There were no hurt feelings, as they knew their time together was up. They counted on nothing, these two, so short-term affection matched their expectations of the world. Their friendship was complete, however, and lasted.

'Mary, doll, I got eight boxes today.'

'Eight boxes, take 'em back, Jimmy.'

'No can do, honey.' His Monday route kept them in touch. Every few months, he called her apartment, worried about some mistake at work, and she'd settle into her sofa giving him as much time as he needed to smooth out the fear.

· *Eighteen* ·

'Kid, I'm home.' What radar was Lawrence using? His timing always coincided with her availability.

'Hi, Lawrence.' Mary said with no enthusiasm, answering the phone over the rack of twenty-four Christmas red velveteen toddler dresses waiting to be steamed.

'Yeah, so listen, I got the condo in Brentwood. Twenty-five hundred a month I gotta pay for three bathrooms. I got six rooms to fuck in. We gotta do it at least six times. What's the most times you ever did it in one day, kid?'

'Lawrence . . .'

'Me, I did it ten times. When I was younger, of course. Now I'm good for a solid three. I need your pussy, Mary. It's nice here. I got a patio – that makes seven places.'

'Lawrence . . .'

'Mary, don't say no. Saturday afternoon. I'm here all day getting sun. What's the problem, we'll fuck and get a tan at the same time. I'll get that nice lean turkey from the deli. Not that pressed shit, the real thing.'

'Turkey's always lean, Lawrence.'

'No, this deli out here, the turkey's better. A little turkey and my dick, Mary. It's hard as a rock. What a boner, right now while I'm on the phone. What am I gonna do with it? Don't answer, I'm saving it for you. Saturday afternoon.'

'Maybe if it's sunny. Customers, I've got to go.'

'Saturday, I'll call you.'

Mary didn't give him a second thought as she poured distilled water into the steamer for the afternoon's work. Martha pulled down the holiday boxes filled with Santa's elves, reindeer, and silver stars and tinsel. Martha was in her element as she prepared for the season of her Saviour's birth and at least one month of unbridled, commemorative eating. Mary's wire of a body worked next to Martha's equally graceful 200-pound mass, as they unravelled hundreds of tiny Christmas lights. It was not an ecumenical store trying to please every faith. Clearly Christian, they pin-spotted light on the infant in the crèche in the window.

Martha worried that Mary would cut her hair now that it curled around her ears. Daily, she praised its length, sheen, and colour. Her latest line of encouragement was her dreams. In a state of absolutely transparent manipulation, she announced to Mary, 'I dreamt you had long hair and you looked so beautiful,' or 'Mary, I dreamt you'd look like Elizabeth Taylor if your hair was longer.' Mary steamed and smiled.

On Saturday she drove to Lawrence's without curiosity. She hoped that seeing him this once would be enough to end it. At least the phone calls stopped after she agreed to the date.

Massive ownership demanded massive security west of Beverly Hills to the ocean. Thousands of locks, grills, gates and codes protected the possessions of the fantasy rich. Mary stared in the camera of Lawrence's condo as he buzzed her through the first set of gates. The street was nice, but no nicer than any other good residential street in any other city. But Brentwood, close to the ocean with perfect weather and protective zoning, was one high rent district.

Lawrence's nasal New York accent ripped through the gentle L.A. afternoon like a siren.

'Mary, look at this joint. Some joint, huh?'

It was lovely, understated and expensive. Lawrence concealed his good taste almost to invisibility with his vulgarity and hotshot bullshit.

'It's beautiful.'

'Yeah, well, I been to Italy. I got the money. What am I gonna spend it on? The deck is upstairs, come on. Fuck the beach. The parking, the people, fuck that. I got everything right here.'

They climbed up a lighthouse stairway to Lawrence's study. Two matching elephant grey leather chairs sat opposite each other separated by a glass desk.

'$2,500 for the pair. Custom made. The desk, $1,500. It's a single piece of glass. No seams, you'll notice. Fuckin' Italy. It took me six goddamn months to get those chairs, but it's worth it. Leather. It's sexy. Put your ass on that, you don't wanna get up. You get more work done.'

Sliding glass doors opened onto a deck with a 280 degree view of the city, stretching from the hills north and East to the southwest silver line of the ocean.

'So, Mary, look, I got everything arranged.' Two plush divans in full reclining position sat side by side with two white bath towels placed on the canvas cushions.

'Why the towels?' Mary asked.

' "A", it's more comfortable and "B", I don't want to get come stains on the canvas.'

'And "C", it's freezing out here,' said Mary, glad she finally found something to complain about in the perfection. Without knowing it, she started her rebellion against Lawrence's tendency to prefer things over people.

'No problem, I got other rooms, Mary.' He flashed her a conciliatory look that was very cute. She turned away to hide the beginning of a smile. Lawrence was small like a jockey. Or a monkey, Mary added in her evaluating brain. They climbed round and round the stairway, as he told her the cost of the finish on the white wood floor.

The sex was efficient. It accomplished what sex, per se, is supposed to accomplish; the momentary release of muscles resulting in ejaculation by the male and involuntary contractions by the female. The minute it was over, Mary wanted to go home. She didn't fake orgasm, she faked feeling.

In all fairness to Mary and her deceit, Lawrence's schedule didn't allow much time for savouring or exploring subtleties of touch or emotion.

'Kid, I want to shoot. After you, don't worry, we'll both shoot. Bang, bang, bang. It'll be re-laxing.' Minutes later, still spurting, he pulled himself out of her, reaching for the towel he'd placed nearby, and started talking.

'That was excellent. Now, you know what I need at Gelson's? I need milk, with acidophilus, sponges, and Evian water. The other waters are shit. You might as well spend the money and get something drinkable. So when am I gonna see you, Mary? We should do this two, three times a week. It's good for us.'

Mary lay on a towel on the floor of the downstairs den, while Lawrence talked and dressed in the adjoining walk-in closet. Mary'd 'shot'. There was no faulting him on that, but her legs ached from keeping up. It was finish-line sex. Winning the race was more important than getting there. A good rule, Mary thought, in sports and perhaps business, having made Lawrence a rich man, but a bad rule for sex, eating, and everything else.

Nevertheless, shooting did have a way of re-ducing anger and the desire to complain, so Mary got up on her watery legs, found her underwear, and listened to the rest of Lawrence's shopping list.

'So, Mary, next Saturday, 3.00, what do you say? We'll relax for an hour and a half, then at 4.30, we'll walk for an hour. Exercise, Mary, we gotta do it. Then the news, and I'll check a result at the track. Then dinner; someplace nice, expensive, you know. Some place with arugula, not those shitty little green salads with one goddamn cherry tomato on iceberg. The crap they try to sell. Jesus, Mary, it gets to me sometimes.

Mary's post-coital calm was drawing to a close. 'What is this, summer camp? What if I don't feel like walking at exactly 4.30 next week, seven days from now?'

'Approximately 4.30. It doesn't have to be exact.'

'Oh, great, what if it's raining, what if there's an earthquake?'

'If there's an earthquake, no walk. It's a deal.'

'Also, I don't want to eat dinner. The sex is okay, but no dinner.'

'No dinner, what kind of a girl are you? Every broad in town takes one look at my car and wants dinner.'

'Take them. What am I going to talk to you about for hours and hours? Sex is the only thing we have in common.'

'That's a good subject.'

Mary had to smile. 'OK. I'll see you at three for sex. But that's all.'

Lawrence had to laugh. 'You strike a hard bargain. If you ever have to do business, you'd better take me along.'

Mary drove out of the locked neighbourhoods back into seedy Hollywood, forgetting about Lawrence instantly. It was always hard to explain to visiting relatives that Hollywood, the township, is a rundown, sleepy, almost rural collection of wooden and stucco houses, off a main street of movie theatres, tattoo parlours, and souvenir shops. The streets have a certain degenerate relaxed quality, and the kind of romance found in depressed seaside resorts trying to remember their heyday.

But the Hollywood tackiness is another illusion, hiding the thousands of ambitious and beautiful faces, guitars, and typewriters all determined to create new dreams. Mary often walked into the barren, Western hills, just blocks above the movie theatres, and listened to the individual rehearsals in each apartment; the recitations, the melodies, the riffs on keyboards and computers – most of it bad, but every once in a while, one clear voice singing above the others a lovesong to break everybody's heart. Mary and the neighbours walking their dogs stand attentive while the anonymous singer reminds them why they keep on going. And they smile and say hello, and for one second open up to each other in the last notes of the perfect music.

· *Nineteen* ·

Just blocks from the sidewalk stars commemorating famous entertainers was the small four storey hospital where Raymond spent twenty-eight of the last forty days. They'd come to learn that the third floor was one of the best AIDS wards in the country. It wasn't good enough to heal anybody, of course, but the quality of care was considered fine.

Raymond lost forty pounds, not enough to put him in any immediate jeopardy, but an indication that he was in decline. The doctors fought each disease as it flared up, but Raymond's body was now host to three fatal infections, serious but in point of fact less annoying than the steady invasion of minor stomach flus, head colds, and rashes.

'I can't eat, Mary. Nothing appeals to me. The antibiotics kill my appetite.'

'Even candy?'

'There is one thing. Could you find me some Salt Water taffy? I had a craving the other day.'

169

'Oh great. That's a good sign.' Should they talk about recovery or give in to death? These were no longer theoretical discussions. They couldn't find the tone. Every visit was goodbye or nostalgia or planning vacations that would never happen.

'Mary, let's go to Tahiti when this lets up. One final blast before I get too sick. Get some brochures. Let's see how much it would cost.'

'OK.' Mary turned the conversation back to the past. It was easier than Tahiti plans. 'Remember that job you got me in the Japanese restaurant. How did we manage to get hired?' Mary brought up the story they both knew by heart.

'Nobody spoke a word of English. I told the chef I'd help him with his golf game. That I have never set foot on the links was not a factor. Remember how he stood in the kitchen practising with his clubs. He wanted to be an American so badly. And you, Mary, oh God, you made me laugh. Remember when you couldn't stand the Japanese music any longer and you poured tea on the tape.

'I snapped. They broke me. I figured they were making up for World War II.'

'And the employee meal. Fish balls in water every night for a year.'

'We threw it on the plants and they died.'

'So we ate green tea ice cream all night.'

'I lived on it that whole year. It was such a nightmare, how come it sounds like so much fun?'

'Because of us, Mary. It was fun because we were there together. Oh God, I don't want to die.'

They never touched much during their friendship. He was too afraid of women and she was too afraid of men, but she took his hand in the hospital.

'Take my strength, Ray. Take it. That stupid Debra said I have a strong electromagnetic force. Take it. She did, and I didn't even like her. I love you. Use my strength. Fight, Ray. Please. I'll get the Salt Water taffy. I think it's a good sign.'

Pauline knocked on the door, gave them a moment, then wheeled an I.V. cart into the room.

'Mary, doll, I've got to change his bottles. This will fatten him up. It's a thirteen-hour food supplement. Predigested, like paté, it goes straight to the bloodstream. We're feeding him all night with this.' Mary looked at Pauline's new red hair. She looked like Clarabell and both Mary and Raymond stared for a moment, stunned out of their tragedy.

'You were thinking Rita Hayworth, right?'

'Identical.'

'I do Gilda later. But that's just for Raymond.'

'I wish it was just for me.' Mary flirted gently, hoping Pauline would understand it was adoration, not desire. Pauline smiled with her ridiculous hair.

'For you, sugar plum, I do Howdy Doody. I want to put a smile on that fox face of yours.'

'Maybe later in the laundry room.' Mary answered knowing she was safe. 'See you, Ray. Salt Water taffy, tomorrow.'

Mary was learning something. Death takes a long time. In extremity, the body fights for life. Even the ones who gave up surrendered long before their bodies were willing to stop. The phrase was 'terminal comfort care', a minimal support approach for those who in writing asked not to be kept alive in a comatose state.

Raymond wasn't there yet, but it was all around him, as he fought to leave the hospital for another few months of life at home. He got a reprieve, and spent time with his family back East and in Los Angeles. He bought a motorcycle and Mary agreed to ride with him down Melrose Avenue. They dressed tough in black leather, and wobbled down the street trying not to play bumper cars.

'This is not my favourite fantasy, Raymond.'

'I have to do it once, Mary. I'm scared to death, but I look good, don't I?'

'Tough. Really. It's the mirrored sunglasses. You look fierce.'

'Good.'

He stabilized the bike for a few more blocks, not as strong as Joanne, but he was dying. Mary hung onto his back, holding him closer than ever before. It was a full body hug and she willed her health into Raymond's skinny frame. She pressed the length of her cheek against the black leather and tried not to cry.

· *Twenty* ·

Mary needed a long night in front of the TV. She lay on her bed in a direct line to the set about nine feet away and watched an unwatchable show. *Circus of the Stars*. Even in her torpor, she found the energy to change the channel after five minutes of some gameshow host being thrown through the air by seven Russian acrobats who smiled at the camera. She clicked through the channels, until a glimpse of Jasmine stopped her hand. Muddy but beautiful, Jasmine ran through the woods glancing backwards to see if she'd shaken the psychotic killer. All was quiet for a moment, when suddenly his gloved hand appeared from nowhere, and clamped over her mouth, filling her eyes with terror.

Mary picked up the phone and dialled her number. It was Mary's turn to make the gesture. The telephone was a cool enough way to get in touch. Jasmine didn't have to know there was any real need behind the call. Neither did Mary.

'Hi, I'm watching you on TV. Channel Five,

the one where you're the therapist and the psycho killer patient falls in love with you.'

'Oh, God.'

'No, you look good. You make that stuff work. I really believe you could psychoanalyze him into not killing you.'

'It's taken my therapist seven years to get me to say no to my mother, but on television I can change a psycho killer's entire life pattern in an eight-minute scene. It's a miracle.'

'And you look gorgeous doing it.'

The girls rested in each other over the phone. It was a pleasure they'd missed. Jasmine knew Raymond was dying, but they let it alone. She thought Mary would cry, and she might catch it. They had cried together often, but only in movie theatres, sobbing out their deeper emotions safely in the darkness, letting an actor or a story take responsibility for their tears. Jasmine didn't like to cry in real life.

'Did I tell you Warren Beatty called me? He wanted to take me to dinner.'

'You're kidding. What did you say?'

'I told him Peter was in the next room with the baby.'

'Did he stop?'

'Yes, he sort of backed off by saying he just wanted to tell me how good I was in *Dual Identity*. First Elizabeth Tate and now Warren.'

Mary couldn't quite answer. It was the first time Jasmine revealed any awareness of the possibilities in Liz Tate's pursuit.

'She called me in Denver. She wanted me to go to Tahiti with her. All on the up and up. She said we could relax. No one would recognize us there.' Tahiti was going to be one crowded little island. Mary kept her mouth shut sensing Jasmine would withdraw like an anemone if she said anything at this moment.

'It's flattering, you know, all this attention. And it's sexy, my God, she has the most beautiful skin in the world.'

'I know,' said Mary.

'She reflected myself back to me. I saw my charm in her charm, my power in her power. It's an identity thing.'

'Narcissism is so fabulous. And it's getting such a bad rap, lately.'

'Well, I didn't go, of course. I mean, it's not like Peter doesn't exist. I couldn't handle it. The drugs. Mary, she's on something twenty-four hours a day.'

'That really amazed me. I've never seen anyone so strung out so beautiful. You're not alone by the way. I would have gone to Tahiti if she asked me.'

'Really?' Jasmine asked in a small, unactressy voice.

'She was irresistible, Jeannie. I saw it a mile off. You were very cool considering the heat she threw in your direction. I got warm just watching. You were inscrutable. What acting.'

'I know. I was born for it. But inside I was out of control.'

'I fell in love with a girl once. Heather. I'm still out of control. I can't get back.'

'You slept with her?'

'Oh boy.'

'Yeah.' Jasmine and Mary were reduced to mono-syllables in the face of the truth. Not the truth about sleeping with a woman, but the truth about how dazzling the right woman could be.

'I'm trying. I'm dating this guy, Lawrence. All I do is think of Heather and I'm all over him. He thinks he's the best lover in the world.'

'Lucky guy.'

'He can't believe his good fortune. I'm always horny.'

'For some girl across town?'

'What's the difference? He's getting it. I'm getting it. It's not a perfect system, but it works. And sometimes, by mistake, when I'm tired, I forget about her and notice him. He's an insistent little guy.'

'Speaking of. Peter's stomping around like he wants some attention. I'd better go.'

'Talk to you later.'

· *Twenty One* ·

Lawrence could barely stop to say hello. He was cleaning his phones. He had a bottle of 409 in one hand and a role of paper towels in the other. Mary stood in the foyer watching.

'The maid does a good job, but still I gotta do it all, Mary. The detail work. Look how many phones I got. Two in the upstairs den. Two in the downstairs den. That's four. One in the bedroom. One in the living room. One floater for the halls. That's seven. One in the master bedroom. One remote, a goddamn $1,500 piece of shit that breaks all the time. One in the kitchen. Oh, and one for the car, another piece of shit, but I gotta have it for the business. I'm not like those creeps showing off. I really gotta have it. I get a call and, bing, I'm there. So, what is that, eleven phones?'

Mary was running a test on Lawrence. She wanted to see how long she could be with him and not say a word, and still be socially correct.

She had a theory it might be years. Not that he didn't notice her, he just had a lot to say.

'Mary, you look so nice. Not like those whores in Beverly Hills. I don't mean real whores, just those women all the time with cleavage in your face. You know me, I like tits, but ten o'clock in the morning over a bagel and they're looking for a marriage proposal. Listen, do something with me next weekend. Drive up the coast. I'll show you some places, not the tourist crap, the good stuff. I know hotels. You'll bring a sweater. You'll get here at 9.15. We'll leave at 9.30. Stop for coffee and a roll at 10.00, 10.15. Get there at 12.30. Browse. Walk. Kill some time. We'll find a nice place to fuck. Some spot on the beach. Or maybe a picnic table somewhere in the park. Now I'm getting horny. Is it warm enough on the deck? I think so.'

Mary always liked cleavage. She thought it was beautiful and feminine and wished she had more of it herself. Mary's cleavage was deepening as she got older, a nice result of her breasts falling a little, and she found herself buying tank tops instead of turtlenecks to show it off. She loved looking at the ample women unfashionable but gorgeous in their lowcut tent dresses. It wasn't a sexual thing, just a pleasing sight.

But Mary was trying to have a boyfriend and decided not to say anything. When he started to tell her what time to arrive on Saturday, her left shoulder hitched imperceptively. Again, she didn't say anything. Was it an invitation or an order? It stung somewhere on the side of her head, but the flattery of being wanted overruled her body's reaction.

They climbed the monkey stairway. Lawrence dusted the handrail on the way up.

'Always a breeze up here, Mary. A hundred degrees and still it's cool. I wash it down once a week. I mean I can't ask the maid. Technically it's yard work. But no yard. I don't want no yard. Grass, dirt, not for me. Look, instead I got these nice trees and plants in pots. A girl comes once a week, throws some water on them, and presto, I got flowers. Simple.'

Mary took off her blouse.

'Oh, Mary, that's good.' His clothes were off in two seconds.

'The approach.' He said as he climbed on top of her. She almost broke her silence by laughing. 'Yeah, well, my technique isn't that great, but it's there, it's hard. It's there for you to use, baby. What do they call it in pornos? My rod, my tool, my dick. Yeah, my dick. You could learn to love it, baby. I do. It ain't as good as a pussy, though. I'd like to be a girl for just one day. You girls can come three, four, five times. Me, I gotta rest, I gotta sleep, maybe eat something. But you, you can come all day. It must be great to have a pussy.' Speaking of, Mary wanted to drift across town to Heather or Debra, but he wouldn't let her.

'Stay with me, baby. I love it. I love it.' Their sunglasses were inches apart. Too cool. Him in aviators. Her in Ray Bans. He knew too much already. She didn't want him seeing her eyes.

'I can't hold it baby. I'm sorry, here it comes.' Bing, it was over.

'Too fast, I know. But that was just a warmup. An appetizer. Give me a minute. Now I'm hungry.' He trotted off, and came back with a turkey sandwich, deli-size.

'Here, half for you, half for me. This is good turkey, try this, Mary. I don't know what to eat anymore. I'm bored. I've eaten everything. Chicken, steak, veal, lamb, what else is there? Oh, yeah, pasta, fucking pasta. Jesus, I honestly don't know what to eat anymore. And P.S. everything's bad for you anyway. Bananas. Bananas, Mary. No good. A study just came out. I go to the store, I stand there for minutes. There's nothing to eat. OK, Chinese. But every night, come on. Truthfully, I don't know what to buy. Macadamia nuts I heard were good. I got ten jars of nuts from Hawaii in the kitchen.'

Mary finished her sandwich and turned over on her stomach.

'Oh, Mary, that's good too. I'm getting a slight boner. Work with it a minute, while I call the bookie. Look at this, my deck phone. I forgot. That makes twelve.'

He started to snap his fingers as the recorded races came in over the phone. 'Stupid horse, he gave up. What are you gonna do? So I'm down sixty shells, big deal. I'll make it up in the ninth.' Mary turned over, as he rubbed her and waited for his race.

'I didn't like anything in the sixth, seventh, and eighth. But Wily Jumper in the ninth, I got a strong hunch. That's it. Mary, open it up, let it go.' He kept one hand on her and one hand on the phone. 'I'm right here. Alright, here we go, he's in good position. He's got a lot left, you'll see. Oh shit, it's a charge, a goddamn charge of the Light Brigade. Six horses neck and neck. Come on, Wily Jumper, hold on, yes, yes, yes. That's it. I told you. OK, I'm up eighty beans for the day. Not so bad. Now I'm gonna pump you right. Not a marathon, but something.'

And he did. Afterwards, they lay there quiet while the breeze from the beach cooled them down. When it got too cold for even the most ardent New Yorker to try to enjoy the California sun, Lawrence stirred.

'I think I'm getting a chill. We'd better go in, sweetie.' 'Sweetie' was new. The sex itself was the only sentimentality in Lawrence's repertoire, until this first endearment. Mary remembered the list of sweet names Heather called her so naturally. 'Darling' was the best, and Mary had been 'darling' from the first, spoken in a tone that implied preciousness and longevity. Being called 'darling' actually turned it for Mary. What started as vengeful curiosity changed to love the second Heather said 'darling' in some casual way. 'Darling, throw me that book, will you?'

'Sweetie' got her attention too, not to the degree that 'darling' had, but still she softened, silently agreeing to the weekend trip in that instant. The secrets to lovemaking are so simple.

Lawrence was quieter as they carried the towels and dishes downstairs, and Mary spoke her first real word of the day when he mentioned the drive again.

'OK.'

'Well, good, that's settled then. 9.15. Next Saturday. Drive safe.'

There was no denying it. Mary got excited when she thought she might have a boyfriend. It was a regular girl's possession. And the phrase 'my boyfriend' certainly went over better in public than 'my girlfriend'. It was fun to say, and now she could speak again to that whole group of women who talk exclusively about their boyfriends. She stuck with Lawrence for at least an hour, smelling him on her arms and hands, reviewing the smaller moments with some clarity. When she stopped to get gas, the Arco station looked communal and friendly, and when the Mexican boys hooted and clicked with their tongues, they were just being boys on a Saturday night. And handsome boys, Mary thought, with their razor haircuts perfectly enhancing their beautiful black oiled hair. She wanted to take one home with her.

· *Twenty Two* ·

Mary used her uncomplicated glow to get some work done. She unfolded the ironing board in her bedroom and pressed her work clothes for the week. She was allowed to wear any top with a children's motif. After a year of seals with balls on their noses, she bought a white turtleneck with Donald Duck heads on the collar and cuffs. The toddlers loved it, grabbing at her neck whenever they came into the store. Martha brought her a T-shirt from Bible camp, with Jesus tending a flock of sheep on the back.

'Jesus had long hair,' reminded Martha when she handed her the gift. There were days when Mary actually wore it. Martha was pleased and Mary disguised her growing enjoyment of Lawrence's bed both from Martha and herself, as she smiled at the customers with a nice neuter spirituality. It also threw people off the track of her more Hollywood nights with Joanne.

She was ironing the Jesus T-shirt when the phone rang late around 11.00 o'clock.

'Mary. Joanne. I've pulled my shoulder out of joint. I need you to snap it back. I can't do it alone. My neighbour's away, nobody's home. It's hurting so bad.'

'It's OK. I'll come right over. Hang on.'

Mary turned the iron off, the answering machine on, and left the house.

Joanne's shoulder was in her neck; Mary could see it immediately when she opened the door. Big, hulking Joanne was crying.

'This is what you've got to do. Hold the arm and elbow tight between your knees. Tight, Mary, hard. You don't have much bulk so use your legs.'

'I'm stronger than I look.'

'OK. Hold it hard. I'm going to twist my body fast, so it clicks back into the joint.' Joanne contained a deep moan as she snapped her back away from the shoulder. Mary held fast, closing her eyes, and heard the bone hit bone as the arm ground into place.

'That's it. Oh God, Mary, it hurts.' Joanne sobbed for her painful life, as Mary held her on the floor, brushing the hair and sweat off her wide, missing link forehead.

'It's OK, it's OK.' Mary whispered and rocked, and Joanne sobbed, 'No, it isn't.'

They sat together like that for minutes, until Joanne realised she was letting someone comfort her and had to pull away. 'Yeah, thanks, it's OK now.'

'What happened?'

'I was changing the light bulb in the kitchen, standing on the stove. Like an idiot, I didn't take the time to get the ladder. And I slipped and fell on my shoulder. It's a weak joint. It goes out easy. It happened all the time when I was a kid.'

The idea of this totally self-sufficient woman hurting herself alone at night pulled at Mary's deepest feelings for the underdog and Joanne's courage to lead an alien life. Mary knew Joanne hurt more than she was willing to admit, when she said Mary could sleep over if she wanted.

'But no crap, Mary. Just sleep. I mean, you drove over here and everything. It's late. Let's go to bed.'

Joanne turned virginal as she asked Mary to turn off the light before she took off her jeans. Mary didn't want to scare her so she got into bed with her clothes on. Joanne was bigger than Lawrence by almost a whole person, but soft. It was an old-fashioned standard double bed. There was no escaping each other as the night got too quiet. A leg touched a leg by mistake and pulled away. Then an arm or hand. Finally, Mary spoke up.

'Look, Joanne, it's a small bed. We're going to touch. It's not sex. It's just touching. It might feel nice. It won't lead to anything except sleep. Nothing more. I promise.'

'Okay. I'm kind of a jerk, huh, Mary?'

'Yeah, well, I've been sleeping with a man lately, anyway.'

'No shit.'

'I can't get you to sleep with me. I've got to do something.' Mary could feel Joanne smiling in the dark, as she eased her bad arm over Mary's waist and said goodnight.

Joanne's morning face was peaceful. It hadn't had time to remember the day might hurt her in some way.

'Well, I'm dressed.' Mary tried for a laugh and got one, lying there in last night's clothes. Joanne, mellowed by sleep, also hung back in bed.

'Look at the morning light,' she whispered to Mary. Joanne's bedroom was like a treehouse. Shuttered windows on three sides allowed more of the outside than the inside to dominate. Scarlet bougainvillea lay in blankets on an extended roof outside the windows. A few tendrils and blossoms pushed one shutter open bringing the colour into the room. Mary watched the city bees and humming birds enliven the foliage with their busy morning work.

'There's a new painting in the living room. You didn't see it last night. I wanna see what you think.'

'Right now?'

'No, but I want you to get up before me, so you won't see how fat I am.'

Mary didn't even try to stitch that wound. Instead she got up and walked into the living room. The painting woke her up completely. All of Joanne's sexuality and passion, so coy and frozen

186

in the bedroom, poured onto the canvas. A naked woman sat with her legs crossed on an upright wooden chair. Totally comfortable in her nudity, her position more the position of someone sitting in a restaurant dressed in a Chanel suit, she looked straight into the eyes of another woman standing across a simple country room. The other woman was muscular, dressed in a very short orange skirt and white blouse, openly appraising the nude, and the nude seemed to welcome it in the most offhand casual manner. The blocks of colour and light were chunky and solid, giving the painting a presence that turned Mary into a voyeur watching this private and mysterious moment. White light poured through a Gothic window on the far side of the room between the two women, illuminating their faces and bodies without shadow. It could have been the light of God or the light of a police helicopter. But it grabbed the eye away from even the bougainvillea climbing into the living room as well.

'So, is it erotic or spiritual?' Joanne asked. Mary controlled her glib tongue this time and let the painting manipulate her senses. It was too soon to answer. Mary wondered if Joanne had finally found her mother, quite literally in the secret moments of the creative act, some memory of love so profound it had to be expressed. Even Joanne wouldn't fully understand the painting once she withdrew back into her daily humdrum self.

'It's wonderful, Joanne. I feel like I'm in the room with them.'

'Good. If you were my lover, I'd paint you nude on that chair.'

'I don't know if I could do that.' It was Mary's turn to get shy.

'That's OK, Mary. We're not meant to be lovers. I was thinking as a painter. You're my little saviour.'

Mary was losing control. She understood the rules when she was taking care of Joanne, but the feeling was too tender when Joanne reciprocated, and Mary might cry.

'I'd better go. I have to be at work at ten, and I look like I've slept in my clothes. Oh, that's right, I have.' This small song and dance got her out of Joanne's apartment intact.

· *Twenty Three* ·

Mary arrived at Lawrence's condo at exactly 9.15, Saturday morning, resenting the early call. It was a holiday with demands. She dressed nicely; white shorts, black blouse, and lipstick, with a royal-blue sweater around her shoulders for style. She knew she woke up with an irritable edge, so she hoped careful dressing would compensate visually for her attitude, which was confrontive to say the very least.

'Mary, you look good,' said Lawrence as he cruised her head to foot opening the door.

'I hope I don't get poison ivy. Wherever we're going.'

'Santa Barbara, Mary. Rich people go there. They don't have poison ivy.' Lawrence seemed willing to humour her ridiculous protestations.

'Santa Barbara. Big deal. It's all hype. The beach stinks.'

'Not where we're going. You'll see, it's nice. And you know me, I been all over.'

Mary tried to ease up and didn't voice the

immediate next logical thought. 'I don't know you. You're a total stranger. All I know is you're a short, fast-talking man who gets on my nerves most of the time.' Instead she gave him a deliberate fake smile and said 'I'm ready' like she was going to the gallows.

He laughed, came right up close, put his hands on her breasts, copped a quick feel and left to check the phone machine. It was a good move and Mary filed it away for later use.

'We'll take the Alfa. It's a $23,000 piece of shit but it looks good, and it drives easy. It's fun.' The car made a horrible noise as they pulled out of the garage.

'It always does that in the morning.' Lawrence stopped the car, popped the hood, tinkered a little, told her it was all fixed, and hopped back in. Mary's door clunked as she tried to shut it.

'You have to slam it really hard. It always does that.' Mary pulled at the safety belt on the passenger side and a bolt fell out, leaving the strap limp in her hand.

'You paid $23,000 for this car?' Mary finally asked and added, 'It doesn't work.'

'Yeah, but look how good it looks. You see it in the movies all the time. It's Italian.'

'Looks is what they're into and it's a beautiful car, but the Italians don't know shit under the hood, Lawrence.'

'Are you kidding, what about the Maserati?'

'Well, okay, but a Maserati's a race car. It comes with a crew of six to fine tune it every day.'

'So, it's got a few bugs, big deal.' Mary lost the fight and tried to settle back and enjoy the ride. He was doing the driving so by all rights the passenger role should have been a pleasure, but she felt his uneasy attentiveness to the car as he listened for hesitations and misfires, and it ruined any possibility of relaxation. If he focused the patience and sensitivity reserved for his car on a woman during the sex act, he could have been a great lover. Three blocks from his house, all the red lights on the dash lit up and the car stalled.

'This always happens, hold on a sec.' He popped the hood again and hit the battery. He jumped in the front seat and the car started right up.

'There's a bad connection. The mechanic can't find it, but it always fires if I give it a good slug. Now we're off.'

It was a long quiet ride to Santa Barbara, interrupted by one point on which they actually agreed. Mary started the conversation, still motivated by her antagonistic mood.

'Malibu's a dump,' she said as they passed the expensive houses pressed against each other like ingredients in a submarine sandwich. Their back doors opened directly onto the slow lane of the Pacific Coast Highway and their front decks surveyed a thirty-foot dab of stony beach between them and the ocean.

'What a hype.' Lawrence added, confirming at least part of Mary's disapproval of everything on the trip so far. His agreement calmed Mary down slightly, and again she resolved to be a nice girl.

Lawrence knew the expensive ropes as he drove past the valets into a beautifully camouflaged parking lot next to the Santa Barbara Biltmore Hotel.

'See, Mary, this is why I gotta have a good looking car. I whip right in, no flack, no discussion. Do this in a piece of shit Toyota and they'd be all over you in ten seconds.' He was right. He parked the Alfa between a forest-green Lexus and a four-door Mercedes sedan. Mary counted at least twenty-five similar cars on either side of the landscaped island. Maroon, tan, black, cobalt, and grey; solid, heavy, serious cars lined the driveway, as the California footmen in their red vests smiled for their tips.

'We're in.' Lawrence cut his New York hustle to a laid-back stroll, and they walked by the bungalows, varied and hidden behind thousands of dollars worth of assorted palm fronds. A two-tiered fountain gurgled gently in the lobby, featuring a Mexican mosaic floor under antique sofas and chairs arranged in intimate conversation corners for lovers and businessmen. The tone and decibel of the hotel staff was quietly gracious, matching the terracotta and buff comfort of the rooms opening into rooms opening into terraces for eating and drinking, all cooled by the perfect breeze bending the palm trees in humble deference to the very rich.

Lawrence stood a little straighter as the atmosphere reassured him there was a reason why he liked to make money. He stopped his incessant talk about pussy as the more elegant influence prevailed.

'So, Mary, isn't this nice. Let's sit for a while and have an Evian water.' A natural blond showed them to a table on the veranda looking across a perfectly groomed lawn to a stone wall separating the grass from the ocean. A few tankers marred the purity of the scene, but a few tankers always seemed to be sitting off the Southern California coast. The promise of offshore oil made these ships a permanent part of the view.

Mary reached for a nut, knocking over her glass of Evian. Lawrence didn't flinch, as Mary, momentarily flustered, apologized for her gaffe. It surprised her. She moved fast but rarely spilled anything, sensing the sequence of moves and their consequences instinctively.

'It's OK, kid, you're nervous. Don't get rattled. They got people to clean it up.' Part of Lawrence was trying so hard to be a gentleman. This was the part that touched Mary, and kept her coming back. That he noticed her nervousness with understanding impressed Mary, who didn't know he was sensitive to her on that level. She was more vulnerable to this man than she suspected, and his tiny emotional generosity caught her attention. He wore his single-ness with an undemonstrative cool, so Mary had to look for clues of affection.

That was the tender moment for the day and it sustained Mary well beyond the point where she started to want to kill him.

Her anger was tempered in great measure by the fact that she had committed all of Lawrence's sins when she pursued Heather. It put a queer perspective on things. Lawrence's need to fuck her fast and quick made sense. It was selfish and thoughtless, but she'd done it. And worse, Lawrence's assumption that she would like what he liked, eat what he ate, follow his lead in an identical shadow pattern, was unfortunately recognizable. He wanted her to be an exact copy of him. It was intolerable. The male–female balance that Mary was looking for was not to be found just because the genders were correct.

Lawrence inventoried the day as it was happening. 'OK, we've had a nice drink, now we'll go for a nice walk for half an hour.' They walked half an hour timed by his watch. 'OK, the walk is done. Now we gotta find a place to do it, Mary.' That segment, as usual, stopped the clock, but only the minute hand, not the hour hand. 'OK, Mary, I'm good for one more after we've eaten. Now we'll eat.' Mary tried to crank up her appetite to meet Lawrence's schedule. Free food; she understood the value of it and wished she was hungrier.

Lawrence was having a fabulous time and Mary wasn't. He had his money, the girl, and the car. But Mary never really liked tourist rhythm. It exhausted her, like being in a museum too long. She either wanted to go much, much faster, zooming to the high points quickly; or much, much slower, resting in a real vacation stupor, waking up only to turn over and put on suntan lotion.

It was a difficult position being angry with Lawrence and empathetic with Lawrence. It was developing into a real pain in the neck. When her throat and shoulder finally pulled too tight to bear, she started yelling. She remembered Heather's even announcement that she wasn't having orgasms, and loved her again for her forebearance and patience. But maybe after all Mary deserved more patience than Lawrence did during this holiday trip. Mary wanted to go home early because she was having a terrible time, but told Lawrence she wanted to go home early to rest for work the next day.

'Mary, it's a kiddie store, it's a nothing job. You could phone it in. What's the big deal?'

If he'd only said, 'Please don't go, I want you to stay,' she would have turned on a dime. She wanted to love Lawrence but he was killing it. Forget Heather, Mary let fly

'You son of a bitch. How dare you put down my job? It's because of that stupid job I don't ask you for twenty dollars every five minutes like some of your other girlfriends. Even if it is a nothing job, I still have to show up. I still have to stand on high heels for eight hours. Eight hours. You don't even know what that feels like, you dope. For eight hours, I have to smile at jerks like you. And you don't even know about the work in the back room, steaming clothes and tagging. I like it, but it's still work. Then you get me out here and think a few free meals entitles you to the fastest sex I've ever had. You treat me like a whore. No kissing, no affection. You lay back, and I have to do all the work. I'm sick of it. I can pay for my own food, you idiot. I like you, I actually like you, but it would be real easy to stop, if you don't start with a little respect. And the goddamn schedule. I can't stand it. With all your money, you live in a prison.

A penitentiary. I'd have more freedom in Alcatraz. Everything by the clock. Forget me, how do you live like this? It's a nightmare, and you don't even know it, except you can't relax for a minute, no matter how it's pencilled into the schedule. I hate you.'

Mary wanted to continue, but she was getting tired and really wanted to go home. Also Lawrence's reaction was puzzling her. He just stood there, and in the middle of the tirade sat on a little bench near the boardwalk where she started yelling.

'High heels, it must be rough. I didn't think of that,' he said in a small voice. Out of the whole speech, she could see his brain dwelling on the high heels issue, reviewing it in his mind, turning it over. He owned a couple of hundred pairs of shoes so feet were important to him, and the high heel complaint penetrated and changed his perspective. It was very sweet to see. Mary sat down on the bench with him, and they looked at the sunset for a long period of unmeasured time. Mary tried to remember she could be angry at Lawrence and not all men, like she was angry at Debra and not all women.

· *Twenty Four* ·

Raymond had spent thirty-two days of the last forty days in the hospital. That left eight days to finish up with his parents. His father was still young enough to have mostly brown hair. His mother aged twenty years in two months. They loved him completely. His death was the problem, not his life, as they rallied with homemade food and stories from back East. Crazy Aunt Gina shot the tires out of the mailman's truck when he jilted her. Baby Terry swallowed a Ninja Turtle doll with absolutely no side effects whatsoever. Raymond laughed with one eye, sitting in his wheelchair. Days after their motorcycle ride down Melrose, Raymond's left side stopped working and he couldn't walk anymore.

Pauline made him a T-shirt that said '20 T-cells and still surviving.'

'He fights, Mary. He won't let me give him demerol or morphine. He wants to know what's happening.' Pauline talked to Mary in the hall outside Ray's room.

'He's sharp as a tack, but his heart is carrying the whole left side now. It's going to get tired soon.'

'Do you have any idea how soon?'

'He's fighting just about as hard as anybody I've ever seen up here, but it might end anytime, cupcake. Say goodbye to him. Tell him you love him everyday.'

'Oh, God.'

'Just tell him you love him. Over and over. And touch him. Don't be afraid. I touch these guys all the time. Hold him on the right side. He can still feel there.'

'Also, Mary, when Raymond dies, a couple of guys are going to come in here with jumper cables and ask you point blank if you want him brought back. They can do that now. They can jolt him back for a day or a week, but he'll probably be in a coma. Your friend will be lying there, and they've got the juice. It's not some bullshit *Newsweek* cover story. It's dealer's choice. And you've got three minutes. Talk to Raymond today. Find out what your friend wants. Get it clear, sweetness.'

Mary walked into Raymond's room and pulled a chair over to his right side.

'Hi, Ray. How do you feel?'

'Better. I think this new drip is making a big difference.' His chest was now permanently connected to an I.V. bottle of liquid food. His bruised arms couldn't take anymore needles.

'Ray, we've got to talk about the outside possibility that your heart could stop. If it does, they can bring you back, probably in a coma, but alive. What do you think?'

'You mean if I die, should I stay dead?'

'That's about the size of it.'

'Or should I pull a Frankenstein. Not a whole Frankenstein, but kind of a thin, wimp Frankenstein who can't walk.'

'Halloween is coming. It might be a good look.'

'Remember the Halloween when you made a pass at me, Mary?'

'I know I was an idiot, but I loved you so much. I thought sex was the only way to show it. You said no so gently. It was the best rejection I ever had.'

'You weren't an idiot. It's just me. It's who I am. It didn't mean I didn't love you.'

'What about the end, Ray?'

'Dead is dead. Let me go when my heart stops. I'll go on the morphine when it hurts too much, but if my heart stops, that's it.'

'You're sure?'

'Not really. I just figure the body will know when it's had enough, so we'll let it stop. As for the rest of me, it's angel time, Mary. I'll be with you every step of the way.'

'Me too.'

Mary drove home high on the intimacy of death. As he was leaving her, they were merging. She was not alone as she picked up her dry cleaning, swept out the garage, and opened her mail. Raymond filled her with his courage and his memories of their short life together. There was no forgetting.

Two days later, Pauline called and told Mary to come right over.

'We've put him on morphine, Mary. He's in and out of consciousness. He still knows what's going on but it won't last long, precious.'

Before dressing, Mary called Jasmine's machine. 'Raymond's pretty bad. I'm at Hollywood Community Hospital. I'll call you later.' Just leaving the message steadied her. The idea of Jasmine was more powerful than Jasmine herself. Maybe there had been too many famous shots of her with the wind blowing through her hair to know if she was real anymore. Mary wondered if this was just an actress's dilemma, or did image confusion sink us all one way or another?

The gay friend was dying. The stereotype could have gone on forever, with the hip talk and the non-aggressive presence, but death was forcing Mary to look harder. She wanted to tell Ray how important he was, how his manliness gave her the musk and the hair and the size without the pressure. She wanted to thank him for showing her how to love without sex. It was hard, like playing a game without eyes, but it sharpened every other sense, and taught her about a love that asks for nothing. She wanted to tell him about his beautiful brown eyes that tried so hard to be haughty with attitude and blue with contact lenses, but could never be anything but tender.

Mary put on a jungle print blouse, wild with pink hibiscus and purple orchids. She painted her eyes deep and sultry and teased her hair. Then she cut the gold thread on a sample vial of 'Quelque Fleurs' perfume she'd been saving for two years, dabbed her wrists, elbows, knees, neck, and cleavage, and drove to the hospital.

'No jumper cables, Pauline. If his heart stops, let him go. That's his decision. His parents know.'

'Right. Looking good, Mary.'

'You better believe it.'

Mary thundered in, dizzy with confidence in her ability to handle Raymond's death. She needed the bluster to push her into the room. When she kissed him on the cheek, she lost her charge. His beard had gone completely white. Until that moment she hadn't noticed. It denied her the memory that wanted him to stay alive and handsome.

Raymond's left eye drifted over to hers slowly as if she'd never left.

'Mary, are we in Paris?'

'No, angel, we're in Los Angeles.'

'It smells like Paris. Remember the flowers.'

'It's me. I'm wearing perfume.'

'Oh, I love it. Are you sure we're not in Paris?'

'Yes, we're in California, Raymond. Hollywood.'

'Home of the stars.'

'Do you want some ice cream? Chocolate.'

'Mmmm.'

Mary opened a dixie cup of hospital ice cream and fed Raymond little bites.

'It's glace in Paris. Glace chocolat.'

Mary's energy evaporated, as the morphine rhythm of Raymond's observations slowed everything down to a happy childlike patter. They held hands and watched the shadow of a palm tree move across the wall opposite the window. It looked just like Rod Stewart's hair.

'I'm getting so tired, Mary. I have to sleep, but I'll come back. I just need a nap, then I'll come right back, I promise.'

'I know you will, Ray. I know.' And he did come back in her dreams.

When Mary finally walked back into the hall, she saw Jasmine talking to Pauline. The actress and the nurse were equal stars in their different worlds and had spotted each other right off. Jasmine looked like a million in movie make-up and hair. She'd come directly from the set. Light from the window at the end of the hall backlit the scene and silhouetted her figure under clothes chosen both to hide and reveal. Movie lighting only reflected what the desert sun did naturally.

'Oh, hi,' said Mary, trying to find Jasmine underneath the spectacular L.A. grooming. Only her voice sounded familiar. She was trying not to cry. 'Hi, Mary, how are you?'

'Ray's gone.'

'I got your message.'

'How did you get away from work?'

'They wanted me to run through a graveyard filled with skeletons celebrating Satan's rebirth. I was looking for any excuse. Oh God, you know what I mean. I'd run through fifty graveyards if it would keep Raymond alive.'

'Skeletons, well, that's about right.'

'Vicious skeletons with snapping jaws, and mud.' Jasmine added.

'Do you think we're being a little morbid?'

'Yes, well, hospitals do that to you. Come on, Mary, let's get out of here. Let's see how fast my car goes. They told me 120, but I want to see for myself.'

Pauline looked up from her console as two attendants from the morgue wheeled a gurney into Raymond's room.

'Go on, Mary, let your friend take you for a ride. You don't want to see this. It's over now. Go on, sweetness.'

'I love you, Pauline.'

'Go on, honey, there's the elevator. Nice meeting you, Jasmine.'

'I don't want to leave him. He's all alone.'

'Come on, baby,' Jasmine said as she took Mary's arm in the same steady way she'd taken her arm when she first showed her a sound stage, and introduced her to Robert Redford as her best friend. This had made Mary feel good for about three years. But Jasmine had called movie lovers and movie children 'baby' in box office hits for a long time. 'Come on, baby' as she pulled her kidnapped son out of a storm drain. 'Come on, baby' as she urged a handsome leading man to undo her blouse. At the moment, it sounded very real and very good, but the phrase reminded Mary of too many film clips to sound entirely genuine.

Mary had a hard time breathing in the elevator. She thought she could overlook the fact that a man had just died while she watched, but it was about to make her faint.

'I think I'm going to be sick.'

'It's okay. Use my purse. It's a prop.' Mary lost a little breakfast on the MGM label. Someone had taken a magic marker and written 'MGM property, do not remove' on the purse's inside flap. Her knees buckled but Jasmine held Mary up with her worker's arm tight around her waist. Eighteen hour days and four a.m. wake-up calls had turned her arm into a machine.

'I can't go 120 in the car,' Mary confessed, ashamed to admit she didn't like speed all that much. It was another macho trait she'd faked hoping to look strong in the masculine world.

'I know. I was just saying that to impress you.'

'I'm impressed enough. You can lighten up with the impressing.' A second wave of nausea ruined the MGM purse for good. Jasmine tossed the bag into a trashcan on the way to the car.

'Wait, what if I get sick again?' Mary asked, worried about the Jaguar's leather interior.

'It's just a car, lamb chop. We can clean it up. There's a barf bag in the glove compartment for the baby.' Jasmine was still there. Her practicality gave her away. Mary had to consider that her friend really meant what she said and that the occasional overlapping of movie and real life dialogue was an occupational hazard.

'Don't go too fast.' Mary repeated as she pulled the seatbelt across her chest.

'Don't worry. I'm in control. It's what they pay

me for.' That was true. Jasmine could drive a car with Clint Eastwood sitting in the front seat. It took an awful lot to impress her into any kind of visible nervousness. Her husband and baby might make her tremble, but show business was just a job. It was the quality that kept Jasmine working long after the other starlets dropped out.

She manoeuvred the car out of the tiny hospital parking lot onto ugly Argyle and drove to the 101 going north. The air conditioning took the edge off the heat, but the midday sun was so bright, Mary's eyes teared up. It seemed wrong for someone to die in the middle of the day.

Mary didn't relax much with friends. It was a state of mind reserved for lovers during those brief moments after sex and before she wanted to go home. But too much had happened for Mary not to give in to Jasmine and her beautiful car. She took a breath.

Jasmine's voice was her own as she laid out the plan. 'We're going to learn bridge, baby. I've started already. It's so complicated you can't think of anything else while you play. The game's got rules just for shuffling. It takes years to get good at it, but I'm sure we can speed that up a little.'

'Bridge? You mean the bridge that ladies play?'

'Why not? Ladies know how to have fun. It's just that no one pays attention to them. Why do you think all those women play bridge once a week? You can eat, drink, smoke cigarettes and talk dirty. And the men leave you alone. They respect the structure of it.'

Jasmine's cure for devastating personal loss was a card game.

'Does Liz Tate play?' Mary asked. It was time to get this out.

Jasmine had been waiting for the question for over a year and answered. 'Liz Tate was a crazy dope addict who toyed with both of us for a while. We were lucky to escape. She's taking prisoners now.'

'Her love is electrifying,' Mary added.

'And it's for life.' Jasmine looked at Mary and asked if she could push the car to 80.

'Why not?' said Mary, as they blasted up the freeway laughing till they hurt at sex and death.

· *Twenty Five* ·

'Mary, ya gotta come over. I gotta new sofa. Black leather.' The phone jangled Mary first, then the voice on the phone jangled her more.

'I don't want to.'

'Mary, what are you saying? A good plough–job is what you need.'

'It's what you need, Lawrence. I wish you'd speak for yourself.'

'Come on.' Lawrence didn't offer to come to her place. He rarely drove east of Doheny, the street that separated Beverly Hills from the rest of the world.

'No, no, no, no, no. I don't know how I can be much clearer.'

'OK, no rush, how 'bout Sunday. We'll go to the movies.'

'No.'

'What, are you kidding me? We'll walk around the mall. Anything you want to eat, Mary. International.

Except for Mexican. I hate that goddamn Mexican food. Then a nice movie. European. An art movie.'

'I hate art movies. Why do all my friends think I want to read a movie? I can't stand that slow foreign crap. I write one fucking poem, and they think I'm erudite. I want to sit in front of the set and watch sitcoms and copshows if you want to know the truth. I say this over and over and no one believes me. They think I'm doing a joke.'

Rebellion against Lawrence was forcing Mary to reveal who she really was. It felt fabulous. The more she wanted to break up, the closer they got. Her irritability seemed to excite him. Mary wanted to write a how–to–get–a–man book. Her first cardinal rules were: 1. Tell them you like women, and 2. Tell them the truth.

'No problem. Come over Tuesday, we'll watch sitcoms.'

'I don't want to see you anymore. I want to break up.'

'Don't be ridiculous, Mary. You need some action, some rubbing, some good hard dick.'

'Goodbye, Lawrence.'

Three days later, as if nothing had happened, as if all was right with the world, as if God was in his heaven, the phone rang.

'Mary, I'm so horny.'

'I'm not.'

'You know, I was thinking, you deserve petrol money. You drive over here. I forget about these things. I'll give you twenty dollars petrol money. It shouldn't come out of your pocket. Twenty shells, what's the difference?'

Mary could have launched into the old 'you're trying to buy me' speech, but she remembered wanting to pay for Joanne's dinner so badly. Part of Mary thought free dinner might buy Joanne. But there were other messages in her offer. Mary also wanted to show Joanne she was solvent, that she wasn't going to become a dependent. Then there was the fact that she adored Joanne and wanted to treat her like a prize.

She spared Lawrence her indignation, but continued to feel he used his money as bait, rather than largesse. It was a hard call. Mary had worked longer hours to afford a pair of earrings for Heather. The gift was meant to keep her, please her, decorate her, and make her smile. She gave Lawrence the benefit of the doubt.

'Tuesday, Mary, Tuesday. It's a good night. No football.'

He literally wore her down. Once again it was easier to say yes than fight. Mary doubted this was love, but needed more information. It was obligation time, as she drove through the electronic gate into Lawrence's condo on Tuesday night. He opened the door dressed for his walk.

'Let's go to the mall for an hour and watch the sunset.'

Everyone seemed to have the same idea as the promenades in the mall filled with people flexing their bodies after work. The side of Mary's head tightened, as she marched to Lawrence's schedule, but she couldn't spend an entire relationship taking a stand.

Lawrence walked in an abbreviated New York style, fast but incorporating the California cruise; the non-insulting open-faced stare that checks everybody out. Mary usually took refuge from this appraisal by concentrating on store windows and her own thoughts. But it was getting harder not to notice. Lawrence's abrasive presence continued to remind Mary that men were out there. They were everywhere. The male visibility, triggered by Jimmy's sweet hazel eyes and reinforced by Lawrence's pursuit, increased as she charged around the cappucino makers and Pottery Barns at the mall.

Even some of the young ones gave her the eye. She saw them through her sunglasses, worn at dusk to protect her more from Lawrence than the sun.

She'd look up for no reason except instinct into the eyes of a Mexican chef, or a well-dressed professional letting her know for one second that they liked her. Sometimes she smiled, and they shared the tiniest moment, no harm done, giving them both a lift in the shoulders, a hint of connection.

'So, Mary, how 'bout we go home and fool around?' Mary wondered if she could have sex with Lawrence without fantasizing about someone else. She doubted it, but it was an interesting concept; thinking about the same person you were having sex with.

Once when Heather and Mary were kissing in the car, Heather pulled away for a breathless moment to say, 'Isn't it sexy?' And it was, because all they thought about was each other. Was it love or the newness of the experience that made it so intense, like the first makeout parties in high school? Mary wondered if he was reading her thoughts as she looked up into the naked appreciative eyes of the mylar balloon salesman.

· *Twenty Six* ·

'They're everywhere, Joanne. The men.'

'I never see them.'

'Now that I'm sleeping with one, I see them all over. Unfortunately, I think I've got the worst one. Can I come over?'

'Yeah.' Since Raymond's death, Joanne eased up on her hand's off policy. She finally seemed convinced of the innocence in Mary's friendship. If they sat together and watched TV, they leaned on each other. Death had moved them to a place where casual touching was precious.

Two days after Raymond died, Joanne made dinner for Mary. Her lumbering presence in the kitchen created a meal that was delicate and specific like her drawing. She served bowls of rice and vegetables on the floor of her bedroom, where they sat inches away from an old black and white TV tuned to a channel showing endless syndicated reruns. Joanne brought little powders and shredded things out of her cupboards. 'Try this on the rice. Try this on the broccoli, try this on the cabbage.

'What are these things?'

'I collect exotic spices. Mostly different peppers and seaweeds. It's salt and pepper with a huge range.' Time slowed to nonexistence, as Mary savoured the new tastes, and Joanne cared for her in the tiniest detail. So many feminine secrets were hiding behind Joanne's burly farmhand appearance.

The existence of men wasn't a good subject for Joanne, so Mary let it lie, even though Lawrence nagged at her from across town.

Mary got a headache whenever she saw Lawrence. She strained to have an orgasm in the two minutes he allowed on his schedule for sex. Mary had become an item on his list. Make money. Buy food. Wash car. Get haircut. Have sex. Brush teeth.

She was also developing a big crush on an exotic lovely in another part of town. Los Angeles was handy for this sort of thing. It was easy to separate lives into the different neighbourhoods. Mary tried to be the bourgeois straight wife in Lawrence's buttoned up rich land of Brentwood. She relaxed in the funky artistry of Joanne's seedy Hollywood. Jasmine took her to the bright fast fun of Tinseltown in the highest hills overlooking the rest. Jimmy linked it all up with his UPS route. And now a sultry beauty, perhaps a Debra clone, threatened to uncover a sensuality resonating with dark immigrant life in the endless flats between the hills and the ocean.

It was a sure sign that Mary needed to kill Lawrence or tell him the truth. She drove to his condo at the scheduled time, after the mandatory pre-call to confirm, sat down on the towel-covered Italian leather sofa, and spoke.

'I'd rather be home watching cartoons alone than spend time with you. The schedule is a nightmare. I have more fun with my worst acquaintance at an obligatory lunch than I do with you. I suppose the things you offer me are nice, but they feel like traps. Every time you tell me to get the towel or take a walk at 4.17, I feel like I'm with Father, or Mother, or Wifey, and I chill. Bone dry. No juice. The sex is gone. Plus there is no affection, not a single physical move that shows any emotional tone at all. You don't kiss me, for God's sake. Either you slow down and talk about love for two seconds, or I've got to go.

'P.S. I've done it. I've dated women. I know how hard it is. I also know I moved heaven and earth to get one. I've sat, and I've waited for the pleasure of her breath on my neck. The fattest, ugliest one was a treasure compared to the crap I'm getting from you. And just to be fair about this, I've been rejected. I've been told I was a lousy lover. I've been told to keep my hands off. I've taken all the manipulative shit that can come down from some of the girls. And I've spent money, when I was poor, and worth every penny by the way. So unless this heats up a little, I mean it Lawrence, with no tears, I am gone.'

'You want it perfect, Mary.'

'No, I want love. There's tons of it out there and none in here.'

'Well, love. I don't know. I do what I can. I pick up the cheque. This is a nice thing. It's my way. I'd drive you crazy if I suffocated you. Like some guys draping themselves all over a girl, needing her every minute. You'd hate that.'

'That's not love, that's possession. I'm talking about love. Pure love.'

'Pure love. Well, that's something else.'

Just the words misted both of their eyes for a moment as they looked to that far romantic place where love once existed in a song or a movie or a dream. They'd forgotten the hope of it. The words hung in the air, sparkling with possibility. They had the energy to quiet Mary's fury, and soften Lawrence's voice.

'I'm leaving, Lawrence. Please think about it. That's all I'm asking.'

Mary's headache was gone. Her neck reemerged from her shoulders as she got into the elevator not knowing what to feel, but knowing she felt better. The music on the car radio sounded richer and more important. Mary sang along a little, and her body wanted to dance. But not big, just a little toe tapping to the sound of her voice.

She was home one hour by the clock, when the phone rang.

'I love you. I love you.'

'Too fast.' She hung up, unplugged the machine and went for a walk. The hills were parched and the deer came out of Griffith Park right into the manicured back yards looking for water in the bird baths and fountains. Mary counted three, two stags and a doe, as she climbed up towards the Hollywood sign. The Japanese tourists stood in the middle of the street, trying to get a photograph of their children and the famous landmark in the same frame.

She hiked to a water tower well past the last house hanging onto the unstable shale of the hill. If it ever rained again, that house was history. The rain and mud would pry it off its posts and send it down the canyon. Everybody knew it, but defying nature was gambling at its most exciting. The water tower stood at a point where three canyons intersected at the base of an unpassable ridge. The city stopped and wilderness began. Mary sat and looked into the brown haze. She was high enough to be at eye level with it. The smog was a new stripe in nature, like the strata in geological digs. The blue desert sky pushed on it from above, and somewhere below was the city, hiding until sunset when the lights came on and identified the patterns of living and traffic that seemed to go on forever.

Live rock and roll with a tough base pounded the walls of the canyon. It was more than a group of teenage boys fooling around in a garage; it sounded great, recordable. That was the neighbourhood. Wild anise, the dominant weed, made the brown air sweet, mixing with jasmine and orange blossoms to die for. Mary could feel the sun oxidizing her hair colour, giving it the desert tinge she'd pay a rich Los Angeles hairdresser to remove.

The ground was bumpy. Even so, Mary lay

down, stretching her arms behind her head. She wondered about snakes in the chaparral, but had never seen one. She rejected the quick thought image that put one slithering up next to her body heat. It was the same real fantasy that put a shark next to her whenever she swam in the ocean. There always seemed to be a dark shadow in the water that could eat her up. She forced her mind back to the fragrant air and sun. It took some concentration. Lawrence didn't even exist, as his little mosquito efforts to get her to come to his house faded to a minor irritation. Mary was tired, and finally dozed in the sand.

'Raymond, you're here.'

'Of course. I told you I'd be back. You know, Mary, you really should hang all the paintings in your apartment a few inches lower. It will look fabulous.'

'OK.' Mary saw her living room through Raymond's eyes, and knew he was right. They sat in Mary's kitchen sprinkling jimmies on frozen chocolate yoghurt. Raymond was muscular again, and he leafed through *The Joy of Cooking*.

'Mary, we have to try Cajun food. Blackened pepper. Have you ever heard anything sound so mouth-watering?'

'Well, candy, chocolate, cake, cookies, petit fours, filet mignon, french fries, to name a few.'

'Pommes frites. In Paris it's pommes frites.'

'What's this obsession with Paris?'

'I don't know. Suddenly I can speak French. I've never been east of Newark, and I can speak fluent French. I knew I was pretentious and grand, but now I've got back up. Call Shirley MacLaine.'

'Ray, I'm still dating Lawrence.'

'It's a long time now. I couldn't string two weekends together with the same person after Philip died. Except that Greg. And on the third weekend, he stabbed me. I know I got on his nerves, but I think stabbing someone is overreacting. Get this. Cajun shrimp with blackened pepper in apricot preserves. Talk about sweet and sour. I'm salivating.'

'Hey, Raymond, how about some music?'

'Something with a beat, Mary. Something with life.'

'*Italian Girls* by Hall and Oats.'

'Perfect.' They danced to the music as Raymond blackened pepper in a saute pan until the kitchen filled with white smoke.

Mary woke up when the band in the canyon stopped playing. She brushed off the twigs and dirt, noticed there was no snake, and climbed down the hill. On the way to her apartment, she stopped in her garage to pick up a hammer. Inside the living room, she lowered all the paintings three inches. Raymond should have been a designer.

Mary's mood buoyed considerably after her dream. Raymond's sweetness calmed her fear, like it had in life, and she reconnected the phone. It rang four times, then stopped, over and over. Mary didn't need a machine to get this message. Finally she picked up. Her terms with Lawrence included giving him a chance.

'Yeah, so Mary, would you come over Friday night? If you're free. And sleep over. We'll do it in the bed, Mary. The bed. I know a new Italian place. It's good. Expensive. We'll eat and go home and do it in the bed, Mary.' In point of fact, they'd never done it in the bed. Lawrence's bedroom was the final frontier.

'OK, I'll be there. But no calls to confirm. I don't want it to be like the dentist.'

'Can I call to say hello?'

'No.'

'Will you call to say hello?'

'No.'

'When we first dated you needed an agent. Now I need a goddamn agent.'

'Bring him along. I'm in one tough mood.'

'Yes, sweetheart. A three-way.'

'Bye.'

Mary spent the rest of the week in the solace of her job at the baby store. Martha took complete credit for Mary's fluffed up appearance. Mary was beginning to hear the men whistle. The new kind of whistling, not wolf calls, but covert little tunes that could be either appreciation or plain whistling. Not only the construction workers but the three-piece boys, right up close when she was standing by an elevator. No longer the girl with the butch cut, who would go into a hamburger place to get something to eat and be called queer.

The big winter sale was coming, and Martha and Mary had to put a red dot on the inside label of every piece of merchandise. This procedure protected them from refunding full cost on returned items sold at sale price. It was an exclusive store and insisting on a receipt just after Christmas was considered bad form. They kept a list of sale prices on each item and referred to it when they saw a red dot. Mary sat with a pile of red pentels perfecting her dotting technique. If she pressed too hard the ink would spread, possibly staining the edge of a white Peter Pan collar. If she didn't press enough, the hard polyester threads of the label wouldn't take the ink.

They kept the back door open so the sun and cool winter air filled the cramped workroom with a fresh holiday energy. Four tiers of racks from floor to ceiling were jammed with toddler clothes in order of size. The ladies kept their arms firm shoving the clothes back one more inch to make room for the new items delivered daily by Jimmy's truck. Martha was strong and able to push much harder than Mary, who stood precariously on the ladder slipping the clothes in fast while Martha held a space open. Martha talked about her four children. Her girls were beginning to date, and she told Mary they would marry young, because they absolutely wouldn't sleep with their boyfriends before wedlock. Her sons might have a little more leeway, but they too would marry very close to the virginal state. There didn't seem to be much rebellion in the children, who bounded into the store happy and athletic, obviously adhering to the values of their parents.

Their support group was evangelical and Presbyterian and Mary could see it was powerful. They weren't bumpkins, but they viewed urban turmoil from afar like stories Marco Polo might bring back from the mysterious East. The children, motivated by religious conviction, certainly did more in the way of good works than many, but they went home to a closed system fortified by friends and neighbours who thought exactly as they did. Part of Mary envied the simplicity of their choices. Mary's conservative nature clashed mightily with a sensuality demanding expression. In the meantime, she found the way to make a perfect red dot. She pressed hard but pulled away quickly. This released just enough ink to mark without staining.

They pulled down, red-dotted, and re-hung about a thousand pieces before knocking off for the last hour of work. Then they stood by the cash register like school kids waiting for the bell to ring. At five to five, Mrs Daladier flew in with two of her four boys, needing red corduroy pants for the holidays.

'Maaaaaaaary.' Arthur screamed, stunned to see her in a different place, and even better, a great place, a place with toys. Mary could see this confirmed for Arthur her magical status, and when she took him by the hand into the back room crammed with teddy bears, rabbits, and Brio trains, he looked at her in a very adult way as if to say, 'How did you get this wonderful job?'

She sat him down at the little table where the children played while their mothers shopped. Martha held a pair of red pants up to his waist, appraising perfectly his size and weight. She could dress a kid at fifty paces with room to grow. Mothers begged for her expertise when it came to fitting their children. Almost nothing was returned when sold under Martha's keen eye.

As badly as Martha and Mary wanted to go home, they knew Mrs Daladier would run quite a tab, so they worked overtime for this final sale of the day. They were paid strictly by the clock in fifteen minute increments, so this extra effort gained them maybe four dollars. Popcorn and soda at the movies over the weekend. They both tagged every dollar at home like they did at work. Martha was a merchant down to her well-padded bone, and Mary, two generations removed from the Depression, still lived in inherited aftershock.

Arthur cried when it was time to go home. Mary got him to stop by crying too. She threw her head down on the children's table and sobbed. Mrs Daladier picked up her cue by saying they'd see each other soon.

'When?' asked Arthur immediately.

'Tomorrow,' said Mrs Daladier, knowing Arthur was a little vague when it came to time. Mary kissed him on the cheek and said goodbye. Arthur turned red then laughed as Mary fell to the floor flushed with embarrassment. Their love scene could have gone on forever, but Mrs Daladier ended it decisively by taking Arthur's hand and telling Mary to come by and pick lemons anytime.

· *Twenty Seven* ·

'Yeah, so Mary, tonight the bed.'

'Aren't you afraid you might get come stains on the sheets?'

'No, that's OK. That's what sheets are for. I don't object. Although you'll notice there is Kleenex on both night tables, if we go for a record. A marathon.'

Mary was getting used to Lawrence's bragging. She knew he used it to turn himself on. They walked around the mall until Lawrence found a bench he liked and they sat down in their usual separate way.

'I gotta hop over to New York for a few days. Some guys want a special filter. They got it in New York, but these guys, they're idiots, they want me to find it for them. What's the difference? It's tax-deductible. They pay me extra for my trouble. Some remake of "Withering Heights".'

'*Wuthering Heights*.'

'Yeah, *Wuthering Heights*. So I'll be gone a week. Can you last? A week with no pumping?'

'It depends.'

'On what?'

'On if you learn to slow down. Have you forgotten everything I said last time?'

'No. As a matter of fact I haven't.' Lawrence put his arm around Mary and pulled her closer on the bench. Public affection. Mary looked at him like he'd lost his mind, but didn't pull away.

'So, we'll sit like this for a while. It's not so bad. I happen to be one of the sexiest men you'll ever meet.'

'Really?'

'Yeah, well, I get lazy. True. And my business. It's murder, it takes my thoughts, but underneath, I'm a sexy guy.' He touched her cheek casually as if by mistake with the hand resting on her shoulder. He let it rest by her mouth for many minutes while they took great interest in the details of the scenery.

'This mall really fills up at dinner time.'

'It's nice. They've done a nice job. With the flowers everywhere, and these benches. It makes you want to come here. It's good business.' Lawrence and Mary shifted bringing their legs in closer. Touching thigh to knee.

'You like these new sweatpants?' Lawrence asked.

'They look good.'

'$18 from $27. Not bad.'

Mary was getting turned on, and she wasn't thinking about anyone else. She moved her head brushing his hand with her lips.

'Oh, Mary,' he noticed quietly. Lawrence was at his best in the mall, close to the things he could buy.

★ ★ ★

His bedroom was sealed off from the rest of the world. Literally. Lawrence had a theory that real Los Angeles air was bad to sleep in, so the windows stayed shut as he stirred the recycled condo air with a ceiling fan. Mary's eyes started to burn. Maybe she'd turned into one of those Los Angeles mutants whose lungs and eyes now needed the toxicity of their surroundings. She also suspected the validity of his premise, and wondered how much actual oxygen was left in the custom-decorated Italian room. She found herself panting to absorb whatever available oxygen molecules still existed.

'Lawrence, please can I open a window? I can't breathe.'

'The air is shit, Mary. I don't want it in the room.'

'Just a couple of inches. I really can't breathe.'

What could he do? The window was painted shut, so they both pushed until it finally budged an inch. Mary put her mouth to the space and inhaled deeply, overloading her system with oxygen like a pearl diver before the big dive. She straightened up, her blood fortified, and hoped she wouldn't pass out.

'OK, Mary, lights off, no TV, just us, let's shoot,' he said as his hands went to the most obvious places.

'Lawrence, where's the fire? Certainly not here.' Mary thought she might have more impact if she spoke in Lawrence's language; scheduling. 'Can we aim for ten minutes of foreplay? By the clock.' She wanted fifteen, but didn't think she should push it. She'd settle for five.

'Of course, naturally.' Twenty seconds later. 'Is it time yet?' he asked, trying for a laugh.

Mary wasn't laughing. She needed to save the oxygen for a possible orgasm. Her diaphram was in place, so she wouldn't have to interrupt the momentum. Mary marvelled at the amounts of plastic she had to insert into her body to have sex with a man. One contact lens in each eye to look attractive and the fist-size dome of rubber to cover her uterus. Some of her friends added plastic breasts and collagen lips. Just once she asked Lawrence to wear a condom to give her a break from the chemicals, and he refused; sweetly explaining he couldn't feel how wonderful she was with that rubber thing on. She didn't harbour any special anger at Lawrence. In her twenties, she'd learned there was not a single, white, middle class male who would wear a rubber more than once or twice. They'd march for abortion rights, but wearing a Trojan was out of the question.

Jimmy always carried one in his wallet, ready to meet her halfway for a spontaneous bang in the park. The teenagers wore them, the military, now the gays, even the really quick boys threw one on to prolong their pleasure, but not Lawrence. He'd put a towel on his sofa to protect the leather, but absolutely nothing on himself to protect his girl. Mary knew this was a rage she had to diffuse. Lawrence was no worse than the rest on this subject. In the world as it was, birth control had to be her compromise. She wanted to take a deep breath to calm herself down, but settled for a little shallow panting.

His timing was bad. He didn't know his move coincided with her furious inner monologue on plastic in the body when he manoeuvred himself between her legs seconds later. She rolled out from under him, fast and strong in her semi-arousal.

'It hasn't even been two seconds, Lawrence. You're so selfish, it's unbelievable. Don't you hear what I'm saying?'

Lawrence tried to smooth things over. 'I know I've got no control. Jesus, you think I'm bad now. You should have seen me when I was twenty-five. I want everything when I want it. This is both bad and good. In business it's good. I don't stand around waiting for the right moment, you know what I mean. I sell, right there on the spot; bing, bing, bing. It's made me rich. But here, I know, too fast, too fast. What a boner I've got. I feel like a teenager. Look at this, Mary.'

Mary knew it without looking or feeling. Her neck and back hurt from the tension of yelling and she felt the rush of guilt from too much anger. She lay back exhausted, too frustrated to hear his apology, and detached from him completely. His hand was anybody's hand. She might as well use it. That didn't work, even though he was trying to tease her back into some kind of presence. She inventoried her girlfriends quickly hoping for a spark, bringing their softness into the room. That didn't work. Old Charles Bronson finally put her over the edge. He snuck into her thoughts with the grace of a ninja and at last Mary sighed, sucking what little oxygen there was out of the room.

Mary wanted out. She nursed the old angers, from birth control to Heather's promiscuity and assigned them all to Lawrence, priming herself for justified escape.

'Joanne, I need you.' Mary cried into the phone when she got home. 'I can't do it. I can't stay with him, day after day. I'm too angry.'

'Mary, come over, I've got layer cake with absolutely no sugar.' Joanne's monotone took the edge off right away. Mary heard escape in Joanne's voice. But Mary was hearing escape in the grocery clerk's 'Thank you, ma'am.' Everyone except Lawrence was desirable and intelligent. She could talk to all of them without losing any composure; tolerant, good-humoured exchanges that implied a humanity and common ground non-existent in Lawrence and herself.

She parked the car on Joanne's familiar rundown street, breathing easy again with the trash and rotting sofa beds sitting on the sidewalk. Life was going to be good now that she was losing Lawrence. A relief.

'I've got company in the living room.' Joanne said as she opened her apartment door. Mary noticed immediately that Joanne was wearing chains and silver tips on her cowboy boots. She was dressed up.

'Mary, this is Mandy. Mandy, Mary.' Joanne introduced her in a voice with more than one note. There was a lilt, a whole new quarter of an octave rarely heard in Joanne's limited range.

Mandy matched Joanne pound for pound, but was the kind of girl who all her life had lived with the phrase, 'You'd be so pretty if you lost some weight.' She was ravishing, with the red hair and white skin of a starlet, all lost on the world, because it was surrounded by two hundred pounds. She looked at Joanne with understanding, occasionally reaching up to brush her hair back from her eyes. Joanne responded. She couldn't get her body to dance; it stayed uncomfortable in the fancy boots, but the impulse was there, as she moved across the kitchen with a lift Mary'd never seen before. Her eyes were still dull, but suddenly attentive. And the corners of her mouth trembled as never used muscles discovered themselves in a smile.

'I have tea from the Philippines, Mary. You want some?'

'Sure, thanks. So, Mandy, what do you do?'

'Nothing special. I sit in front of a computer all day. Data entry.' Mary thought it was too bad only a computer looked into those green eyes for eight hours a day, but maybe that was changing. Joanne brought Mandy a fresh cup of tea, and the sure connection of true lovers settled the room into the present tense.

Mary was going to leave Lawrence. That had been decided. But watching Joanne and Mandy find each other reminded Mary that something was at stake. Mary and Lawrence fought for a reason, but for the life of her she couldn't remember what it was.

Mandy read her thoughts when she said, 'Joanne tells me you're trying to have a boyfriend.'

'Well, after a fashion. I've got a crush on an Armenian girl, who doesn't speak a word of English. She's just a pair of eyes at the fruit stand. She doesn't know I'm alive. So in the meantime, I date a guy, yes. Say hello to Joanne's confused friend. If you're a political lesbian, you'll hate me for seeing a man. If you're a straight housewife, I'm the ultimate threat, the out clause from your husband on a bad day. In between, yes, I date a man who I hate both personally and on principle. I've really found the worst of both worlds. It's Joanne's fault. If only she'd have slept with me, I wouldn't be in this mess. Joanne's the best, by the way. How did you meet?'

'I was temping at Tristar when Joanne slunk by on her way to the basement. Nobody ever knows I'm gay, or straight, or anything, they just think I'm fat. So I asked her to lunch, did a confessional in the mad hope that she'd like me, and she did.'

'Yeah,' said Joanne, summing up falling in love with her usual brevity.

'Well, that's great. I won't go into a jealous frenzy now. I will later, Joanne, you can count on it. But in the meantime, I'm so happy somebody's happy. So how 'bout I stay with you for the evening. We'll rent three or four movies and I'll talk during all of them. Don't worry, Mandy, I'm just kidding. Let me finish the Philippino tea and I'll be going. Boy, it's got quite a kick, I can't stop talking. It's either the tea or my loneliness. My boyfriend's impossible, but I don't want to sit in my apartment alone for another two years, you know what I mean?'

'Ease up, Mary. Sit with us awhile. You don't have to leave right away.'

Mary didn't ease up at all, but the complaining helped. Lawrence had become a giant in her psyche, squeezing her out. With every negative remark, he got smaller, until she found herself again in the company of women.

The phone didn't ring for a while. Lawrence wasn't stupid. In the middle of the bedroom inaugural, he'd whispered ferociously in her ear, 'Why aren't you with me? Why don't you want to sleep with me anymore?' She hadn't answered, and for that moment he let her go. When it came to Mary, his senses were sharper than she thought.

When he finally called, there was resolve in Mary's voice. Lawrence heard it and Mary heard it, surprising herself. She wasn't stalling for time or asking for love; she didn't want to see him anymore. It wasn't a small stand that would cave in by the weekend.

'Kid, I can't see you anymore.' She used the endearment to soften the rejection.

'What, again? Every week you can't see me anymore. Listen, I heard about a new Chinese place downtown. Fresh fish. Fish, I don't know, but I'm sick of everything else. It's good for you. A little halibut or sea bass. They do it nice, I heard.'

'I can't go, I'm sorry. I wish you the best, but I can't see you anymore. It's not working.'

'Fine, if that's what you want. It's your decision.' A peevishness crept into Lawrence's tone, as he made the break up her entire responsibility.

'Lawrence, it hasn't been that great for you either. All I do is nag at you.' Mary tried to include him in the breakup.

'I don't do that to you.' He defended himsclf.

'I know and that's a nice quality.' It wasn't such a terrible thing to praise Lawrence when she never wanted to see him again, but Mary felt like a hypocrite. Every rejection she'd been part of started with some form of 'you're a wonderful person, but . . .' or 'it's not you, it's me.' Well, it is them and they're not that wonderful, so who's kidding who here.

'Look, I've got to go. Good luck with every-thing.'

'When you miss me enough, you'll give it a grab. I give you ten days, max.'

'This is what I'm talking about. It's just a jerk and a pull to you, Lawrence.'

'I like being crude.'

'I know.'

'A jerk and a pull. Now I'm getting a hard-on.'

'Lose it, Lawrence. I can't do this anymore. Goodbye.'

Mary hung up. She always liked sexy talk and it's flare-up during this last conversation robbed her of the finality she wanted.

The relief did kick in, however. It took under a week.

· *Twenty Eight* ·

Mary focused on her job. Not like in romantic fiction, where one's work after a breakup is doctoring or writing or finding the cure for cancer or being a newscaster. As Lawrence had pointed out, there wasn't a career vying with her personal life. She was a salesgirl four days a week, moonlighting as a babysitter.

She broke records at the store, tagging hundreds of infant sleepers at a sitting. 'Let's unravel the Christmas lights,' she suggested in the middle of April, while dusting a display shelf near the ceiling, where even Martha didn't go.

Mary was adamant about not staying in her apartment for two years. Most women she knew, both friends and customers at the store, referred to their husbands as 'him' and men in general as 'them'. Mary kept her discovery to herself, but she was just noticing the specifics of the gender. Like hunting for seashells, it was an acquired vision. Age, weight, and appearance, the usual standards that determine visibility were overlooked, as Mary began to see the men in three dimensions.

Everybody in her generation had had so much sex, Mary figured the occasional conversations between men and women might be a new thing; attempts at communication without the sole motivation being getting laid. She was still shocked whenever a man said something smart or helpful, but increasingly she heard the deeper voices whispering to her when they had the courage.

During lunch hour at the health food store, she listened to a particularly obnoxious man telling the dried fruit salesman what he wanted. He must have said 'without pits' 4,000 times, reminding the salesman of his superiority and condescension during this minor exchange. Even as Mary browsed she could hear this bully's voice talking too loud to make his presence felt. She made the mistake of touching a carob candy with her hand in one of the self-service bins, and he swooped down on her, eyes glinting with joy that he had found a victim for his particular riot act.

'Don't ever touch the candy with your hands. You have to buy that one you just touched.'

'I don't know what came over me. I don't usually do that.' Mary lied, trying to smooth things over, as she smiled politely at a human scourge, the kind of person that even the most peaceful soul would want to kill on sight. That was not good enough.

'Do you know why you shouldn't touch?'

'Because the germs on my hand will get on the food and poison it.' Mary answered with the long-suffering rote of a student who had left the teacher in the dust. His face turned ugly when she didn't grovel enough. Mary took the edge out of her voice, as she realised he was the kind of man who would beat his wife and children into submission.

'Look, I'm sorry. I won't ever do it again.' She exaggerated slightly, when suddenly the dried fruit salesman, six feet tall and smiling at her, quietly interrupted from farther down the aisle. 'You don't have to apologize.' Mary looked up into eyes that sparkled at her resistance as he walked forward establishing himself as the biggest body in the store. It wasn't just an assertion of male strength. He was on her side. She gave him a nod. Daddy, daddy, what a guy.

It wasn't a true dialogue but Mary went back to work with her dislike of the first man balanced by her respect for the second.

She didn't know if the store mothers even cared about her personal life, but with a sixth sense they asked Mary to babysit on all the nights when relationships normally happen. Fridays, Saturdays and Sundays were filled with bedtime instructions and maps to museums and zoos and birthday parties at the Gymboree. Mary had very little time to get lonely. The negotiations with the other side continued, but not with the men themselves. Mary was now confronted day in and day out with their sons.

When the phone rang, Mary was watching Richard

Green in the 1950's serialized version of *Robin Hood* for television. Mary always wanted to be Robin Hood. She never, ever wanted to be Maid Marian. Mrs Daladier interrupted Mary's appreciation of the merry men by sobbing into the other end of the phone. She assumed Mary would know who she was, and spoke without introduction.

'Arthur is flunking second grade. He just got his report card. He got an F in reading, writing, and arithmetic. He's seven years old and his life is over.' Mrs Daladier cried for a few minutes while Mary reassured and confirmed that Arthur was smart. Arthur was smart and underneath her frustration, Mrs Daladier had a plan.

'Listen, Mary, Arthur loves you and you always read and talk so well. I'll pay you some decent money to tutor him twice a week. That damn TV. It's killing my children. They can hook up a VCR to the toaster, but they can't write a sentence. And that stupid teacher, she couldn't care less, and why should she? They pay her two cents a week to teach twenty-five children, half of whom can't speak English. I'm the big liberal. I'm the only mother I know who really believes in integrating the kids. I could afford private schools, but I believed all that stuff in the sixties. The blacks, hell, I wish Arthur was in school with the blacks. We know each other, but this. This is Koreans and Filipinos and Japanese. He's a head taller than the other kids. He's the big stupid white boy.'

Mrs Daladier's tirade was not about to wind

down, so Mary listened for as long as she could, then interrupted hard with, 'When should I start?' She needed the money.

'Today, Jesus, last year, Oh God, I'm really ranting. How about today at 5.30, after work and school. Just teach him to like reading, Mary.'

Arthur was a big white boy. He stood in his room, his white and blue parochial school uniform filthy from just getting through the day. Mary's only edge was that Arthur loved her. The rest of him was a giant loaf of passive resistance.

'Arthur, you're one of the smartest boys I know. You could be at the head of your class.'

'No, I couldn't.' Arthur said these sad words with some feeling. Already he believed the reports about him.

'I've brought you a book called *Swiss Family Robinson*.' Mary held up an abridged illustrated version. They sat on his bed making room among the green piles of Ninja Turtle sheets, pillows, accessories, masks, comics, ooze containers, and pizza catapults. Arthur leaned against her, careless of his body, looking at the first picture of a shipwreck on a reef. Circling shark fins caught his eye, as Mary knew they would.

She read in a quiet voice, hoping to still the pressure they both felt to make Arthur a good student.

'What's a musket?' Arthur asked, hearing the word for the first time, and walking into Mary's trap. She knew what boys liked.

'A big gun, like a rifle.'

Arthur's silence was permission to continue and Mary read for an hour without complaint.

Two days later they recommenced at Arthur's desk. They sat side by side on two hard wooden chairs. Arthur had to practise cursive writing.

'Why do I have to learn this? Why can't I print everything?'

'I don't know, but they won't let you into third grade without it.' Mary wished she had some important answer, but Arthur seemed to respond to her practical approach. He started to write, tracing first a model of a word, then copying the word. She hung with him breath for breath on every curve of every vowel.

'I hate "m"s,' Arthur said, as he broke a sweat over the top of his nose.

'Yeah, they're rough. Go slower.'

'Slower, no, Mary. I don't want to be like one of those kids who has to write slow while everyone else waits for him to finish. They look stupid.'

'I know, but here you can go slowly. No one is watching. If you go slowly here, you'll be able to go faster in school.'

Again, Arthur listened, drawing each 'm' out of the air and onto the page. The 'm's wandered with no knowledge of sitting on a line or starting at a margin.

'Touch the line, Arthur. The bottom of the letter has to touch the line.'

'Why?'

'That's what it is. That's the rule.'

Arthur wiped his left hand across his mouth, and

bent over the paper again. Mary went inside each letter with him. 'Touch the line, touch the line, touch the line. That's too big a space. Do it over.'

Arthur's idea of erasing was to smear the rubber over the mark one time.

'Not good enough, babe. Erase the whole thing. Teachers hate those smudges and so do I.'

'Don't call me babe.'

'OK. That's better. Now touch the line, touch the line. Two more words and you're done for the day.' The instant the last word was written, Arthur made a break for it, but Mary pulled him back and told him he had to put the homework in his knapsack for the morning.

'This is called organizing. It's the most important thing. You do it so you won't lose your homework. What's the first thing you do when you get to school?'

'Get out of the car.'

'Arthur, give me a break. What's the first thing you do with the homework?'

'Make it into an airplane and throw it at Gavin.'

Mary was pleased that Arthur was playing. She was afraid of her own strictness, but Arthur seemed to know it was for a limited time, and teased her back into their old ways.

'Right. Now, what do you do with your home-work?'

'I forget.'

'Put it in the teacher's basket. Say the words.' Mary jumped on him, pinning him to the floor. 'Say the words, or die.'

'Put it in the teacher's basket.'

'One more time.'

'Put it in the teacher's hat.'

'One more time.'

'Put it in the teacher's ka-ka.'

'That's right. Now you've got it.' She let Arthur escape, and joined Mrs Daladier in the bedroom. She was clipping coupons on the spot where Mary had first allowed Jimmy to enter her body. It was a comfortable room where children slept off their flu, and parents had procreative sex, and Mary tried to find the masculine in someone other than herself.

'How's he doing?' Mrs Daladier looked up

'Pretty well. I'm surprised he listens to me. He does everything I tell him to do. He's really trying.'

'He adores you, Mary. I wish I knew how to talk to him the way you do. He's an odd little guy, isn't he.' Mrs Daladier spoke with the wonder of having given birth to someone different than herself.

'He was a gift, you know. I was over forty when I had him. The doctor told me that I couldn't have anymore children after Weston was born. Then eight years later I was pregnant again. I thought George, my husband, would go out of his mind with joy. We both wanted a bigger family.'

'Now you've got Arthur.'

'An illiterate, who can't compete at the second grade level.' Mrs Daladier was obdurate in her bleak vision of Arthur's future.

'No, I can fix it. I'm sure I can. Don't worry. You've made him a good boy, but I can show him how to study.'

When Mary finally left the safety of the Daladier bedroom, she took one phrase with her, 'odd little guy'. She'd never thought of a male as being an 'odd little guy'. Mrs Daladier's observation had separated one out of the mass. Mary had often thought of herself as an 'odd little girl'. It reminded her that she was unique, perhaps rare, singular, and noticed. And in the glow of Arthur's healthy normalcy and his mother's doting, the phrase implied not a deviation, but rather an individual. That a male, even one of the small, non-threatening ones, could be a character, a certain kind of fellow, illuminated Mary's evening. It was a thin line Mrs Daladier had thrown her, but it held and Mary put more weight on it. Partnership could exist with an 'odd little guy'. An odd little guy could collect stamps in one room while Mary watched TV in another. And maybe they could merge in the adult way, like she and Arthur did in the innocence of their schoolwork. Because Arthur and Mary did merge. When they sat together bent over the curve of a 'c', their concentration was one. They both felt it, and resented intrusion. Even the beloved mother was too talkative, too loud for their moments in the glare of the study lamp. The difference between a comma and a period was the only thought in both their heads, as they read and wrote sentence after sentence. They gave each other the flu week after week, passing it back and forth in the shared air over the desk. Arthur used one Kleenex after another, still not completely good at blowing his nose, and they both coughed into the hands that shared two pencils. They farted, Arthur laughing at each tiny burst, while Mary made a big production number of opening the window, and gasping for air.

At the end of the month, Arthur had an English test. They crammed for it, learning by rote the adverb, adjective, and noun. Arthur lay on his bed, holding a grey, fur dolphin, while Mary shot him word after word to identify and spell. She remembered her father doing this for her in the random moments when he wasn't working. 'What's seven times eight?' he'd ask ten times a day, until fifty six was so sure in her mind, she could afford to joke and answer 'two' or 'a million' like Arthur did when he got silly with his newfound knowledge. The taskmaster father could not be denied, as Mary saw in herself the person that would teach the child Arthur how to survive in school. Friday came, the day of the test. Like her father before her, she took the pressure off at the last moment to relax the boy.

'And if you flunk, big deal, it's not the end of the world. We'll study more. I like blowing my nose 4,000 times a week.'

Actually Mary forgot about the test during the course of her day at the store. Fifty velveteen princess dresses had to be steamed, and the fifty satin sashes that went with them needed ironing. Mary drove home with her hair curly from the steamer. Martha had remarked that it looked cute, and would be even cuter if longer.

'My girls would kill themselves for your curls.' She said reinforcing her approval.

At six o'clock, the phone rang, and Arthur's stuffed up little voice at the other end, said, without introduction, 'I got an A. I only missed one, and that's because I wrote down the wrong answer. I really knew it in my head.'

'An A?'

'Yep, an A.'

'You did it. I knew you could do it.'

'Yeah, well, OK, see you next week.' The phone sort of dropped as Mrs Daladier swooped on the line. 'Isn't it fantastic, Mary. He got an A. You did it. I'm so happy. Please come over for dinner. We're having orange ruffy. The kids hate it, so there'll be a lot. You should see him. He's just bursting. He hasn't gotten an A all year. Now he wants to learn chess. He's in with the other boys. Thank you so much. Oh, God, this is so great. Listen, I'll talk to you later, my other phone is ringing. Bye, dear.'

Arthur's A surprised a few people. Another mother heard of Arthur's rise, which continued well into the next semester when he was chosen 'Student of the Month'. She called Mary, hoping for an hour for her Christopher. The divorced Mrs Munson had found a new man, and Mary discerned quickly that she was torn between him and her son, a sullen eight-year-old, who disliked everyone but Mom, who was busy. When Mary met Mrs Munson, she understood why.

Mom was a Valkyrie. Mary remembered this word from Viking history to mean a tall stunning blond woman who one met in heaven. Mrs Munson's mythic looks inspired Mary to look up the word in the dictionary. There she found, 'Valkyrie: chooser of the slain, one of the Maidens of Odin who chooses the heroes to be slain in battle and conducts them to Valhalla.' Mary saw for herself that Mrs Munson could be a consolation prize for death.

No wonder Christopher could not separate from this vision. Mrs Munson was six feet tall, and proportioned for the Olympic games; powerful, muscled, and sleek. Awards and trophies supported Mary's first sidewalk impression, reflecting city and state champion status in volleyball and basketball. But a jock she was not. Blond hair to her lower back put her into centrefold competition, and Mary supposed Christopher vied for his mother's attention with every male in a city wide radius. Both mother and son wore glasses, but because of their size, this was one case where glasses were just pieces of equipment and didn't integrate into the personality. They sat on their noses like Clark Kent's ready to be tossed aside and replaced by super powers.

Mrs Munson and the boy had just moved into Bill's town home. Mary made the mistake of calling it a duplex, letting the hem of her Eastern background show, and Bill corrected her with the phrase 'town home'. Bill filled every inch of his town home with an animal's presence after winning Mrs Munson. He was a full head shorter, but pumped to full width underneath his pinstripe shirt and suspenders. The tassels on his correct loafers trembled a little when he looked at the oversize mother and son standing in his kitchen and dining area. The weight room upstairs, with state-of-the-art equipment, was used often by this man. He showed it to Mary, standing taller than he should to graze Mrs Munson's shoulder.

Mary knew the stance. Heather, inches taller than Mary, had introduced her to the shorter lover's pose; the extended spine and neck, never allowed to slump, ever vigilant in the range of the beloved. Desi Arnaz had it with Lucy.

During Mary's first meeting with the new family, Bill made himself a booster shake from the powders in the cannisters on the kitchen counter.

'Protein supplements,' he explained to Mary. 'Want one?'

'No thank you,' Mary declined. The gym and protein shakes were for Bill. One would need some weight to pin Mrs Munson to the bed.

This was just a first meeting to see if there was simpatico between Mary and the boy. There was none, but Mary didn't push. Christopher sat in front of the TV and VCR in his bedroom prodded by Bill to say hello without shifting his eyes from the set.

'He's a happy kid. I gave him his own complete entertainment unit when Vanessa moved in. We put him in a school close by, and they said he doesn't have third grade level penmanship. We were hoping you could coach him up to par.'

It was a literate house. The living room was lined with bookshelves, neat and new, both the shelves and the books, like Brentano's. Mary just saw books, she didn't have time to focus on titles. A fresh uncracked copy of *Harlot's Ghost* sat on the coffee table next to *You Just Don't Understand: Men and Women in Conversation* and *When All You've Wanted Isn't Enough*.

'I'm sure there won't be a problem. It just takes practice.' Mary didn't express the fear she felt for this little boy, who had given her a look of hatred over his glasses. They made an appointment for next week, and Mary drove home with her scant first impressions. It was a wound-up household. Every room except Christopher's seemed to have it's own theme of self-improvement, with its kitchen of supplemented foods, the dominant gym, and the coffee table piled with self-help books. Mary didn't know the half of it. But there was also a sweetness behind Bill's eyes and pure terror in the mother's, so Mary figured the situation to be a strenuous period of adjustment controlled by this big glum kid.

Raymond was dead, Joanne was with Mandy, and Jasmine was doing Arsenio, so Mary's sources of love were depleted. She thought she was going to have to take on Christopher alone. But there is something about the nature of friendship that keeps renewing itself. Like water seeking its own level, loneliness doesn't rest until it finds solace. Mary started talking and friendship emerged in the form of Mrs Daladier.

'It's really nothing, and I'm sure I can handle it, but I have this new kid to tutor. He's hurt, I know he is. But he's in armour. He won't talk, he won't smile, he won't cry. He just watches TV hour after hour. And he's big. I don't think he'll do what I tell him. He's not like Arthur who wants to do well in school. I don't know how to get to him.'

Mary was hopping up and down at Mrs Daladier's kitchen table after working with Arthur. The other children sat around doing their homework.

Mrs Daladier's daily monologue stopped. Even the constant corrections of the children's behavior slowed to only the major breaches of conduct. 'How many times have I told you to put the top on the juice, Weston. This is not a pig trough.' She listened to Mary. As Mary wound down, agitation showing on her face and in the actual wringing of her hands, Mrs Daladier quietly said, 'Children can be scary.'

That was all Mary needed. She wasn't alone and it wasn't her fault. Children could frighten grownups. Even Mrs Daladier, the mother of the world, allowed this to be true.

'You'll be fine. Call me or George if there's a problem.'

George, Mrs Daladier's husband, came through the kitchen door on cue. Until recently, Mary didn't notice husbands. No wonder wives liked her so much. He was the other half of the four children sitting at the table. Both he and Mrs Daladier were thickening together. Neither of them really had a waist to speak of, but their vibrant middle-aged sexuality enlivened the room, and Mary and the children basked in the energy of the parents' nightly reunion. The Daladiers argued to hear themselves talk.

'Darling, it's insanity to park next to the sprinkler,' he said in passing as he kissed the youngest boy. 'Hello, sweetness.' George was Australian and bursting with expressed adoration for his kids.

'The sprinkler is broken, George. It doesn't matter where I park the car.' They both acted out the respective difficulty of their days, competing for the role of the most exhausted one, as they cooked, compacted garbage, corrected homework, threw in a load of laundry, and drank a beer.

· *Twenty Nine* ·

Mary was watching *Seven Brides for Seven Brothers* when Mrs Munson called to alter the plan entirely. Now she wanted Mary to live with Christopher for four days and guard the town home while she and Bill attended a seminar in Santa Fe, New Mexico.

'It's called Encounter, Mary. It's changing our lives, but we have to do the whole thing or nothing. I'll pay you whatever you want and you could tutor Chris while you're here.'

The town home was nice, the gym equipment was tempting, and the salary would pay Mary's car insurance bill. She could be a mother for four days. They arranged for Mary to pick up Christopher at his new school on Friday afternoon.

'He won't be any bother. He just stays in his room and watches TV. If he gets bored, rent a couple of videos. You might play cards with him if he asks. He likes to play cards.'

Bill and Vanessa were a perfect couple on their way to becoming a more perfect couple. The stay was organized to a fault; back-up phone numbers, hospital and prescription cards, stocked cupboards and refrigerator. Christopher only ate tunafish, macaroni and cheese, and fruit. But he could have McDonald's once and Pizza Hut once during Mary's stay. One coke slurpy, one soft licorice, and one set of basketball cards at 7-11 were allowed after school on Friday.

Only Christopher, sitting alone in front of his Game-Boy, a mass of eight-year-old confusion and malcontent, troubled their perfect California life. At three o'clock on Friday Mary sat in her car in the school parking lot.

'There she is,' Chris whispered to his friend 100 feet away. Mary read his lips and eyes in her rearview mirror, and braced herself, as he crossed the schoolyard. She opened the car door from the inside, and quietly said to him, 'How 'bout we go to Las Vegas and win a bundle?'

His eyes opened a bit, and he laughed, 'Yeah, alright.' Two points for Mary. Instead they went to 7-11, where Christopher comforted himself with his Friday ritual. 'It's T.G.I.F. day,' he repeated a few times, having heard the expression somewhere, but he was just imitating the general sounds of the letters without knowing what they stood for. Mary let the lesson go. She had a feeling kicking back with this boy was more important than dotting every 'i'.

Christopher went directly to his room where each half-hour was marked by a change of show or channel, while Mary settled in. The master bedroom didn't stir her like the Daladier's. The mattress was hard as a rock. It was like lying down on a stretch of pavement. The bed could support Kama Sutra positions and perfect posture, but it wouldn't allow drool or bad breath or head colds. Mary's hips hurt just from the testing, but the room was hotel clean and Mary opened the Levolor blinds to scan the close-up backyards and panoramic sky and hills of the San Fernando Valley.

Napping was out of the question on that bed, so Mary went downstairs past the cartoon voices coming from Christopher's room to look at the books. She'd taken this job hoping that all the wonderful, clean new books would balance out whatever difficulties she might have with the child.

Mary tilted her head to one side and started reading the titles: *Creating Well-Being, Love, How to Survive the Loss of Love, What We Talk About When We Talk About Love, Styles of Loving, The Art of Loving, Women Who Love Too Much, Meditations for Women Who Love Too Much, Kundalini, Relationships: The Art of Making Love Work, Right Use of Will, A Consciousness of Wealth, The Magic of Encouragement, How to Teach your Baby to Read, The Nature of Personal Reality, The Courage to Heal, The Power of your Other Hand, The Road Less Travelled, You Can Negotiate Anything, Shared Intimacies, The Art of War, Situational Anxiety, Managing Yourself, Know your Own Mind, Loving Each Other, The Aerobics Programme for Total Well-Being, One Day At a Time, Mere Christianity, The Problem of Pain, A Guide for The Advanced Soul, The Drama Of the Gifted Child, Tae Kwon Do, A Course in Miracles, Creating*

Money, The Art of Sexual Ecstasy, The Memory Book, The Kama Sutra of Vatsyayana, The Personality Self-Portrait, Staying Well with the Gentle Art of Verbal Self-Defence, Full Catastrophe Living, Control your Dreams, Working with Difficult People, Brain Fitness, Flow: The Psychology of Optimal Experience, Journey of the Heart, Commentaries on a Course in Miracles, Fire in the Belly, Shopping Smart, Climb your Own Ladder, Choosing and Changing, The Complete Stories and Poems of Edgar Allan Poe, Recovery, The Five-Minute Phobia Cure, Skills for Success, A Book of Angels, The Success Factor, Twenty Minutes a Day to a More Powerful Intelligence, Thinking Better, How to Make a Speech, How to Work a Room, The Plateauing Trap, Take a Chance to Be First, Cutting Loose, Strategic Selling and *Winning By Negotiation*.

Mary flipped on the downstairs TV and joined the boy in a little low pressure syndicated viewing. It was that or *The Complete Stories and Poems of Edgar Allan Poe*. Mary was exhausted from reading just the titles of the work books; but ecstasy, wealth, fitness, and love held as much promise for Mary as anyone, so she tried not to judge. Wasn't it sort of touching that there were so many how-to books about love? Sweet Mary tried to accommodate the thousands of pages of lectures lining the room. Another more rigorous, disgusted part of Mary raged at the kindergarten mentality that was going to explain with its crayons and workbooks why everybody was doing it wrong. Mary was vulnerable to catching the diseases some of these books had created in order to sell the cure.

Rich was fine, but Mary suspected only the writers were getting there, as the duped public spent their money on easy promises and fast answers. The snake oil was thick on these modern shelves. Fitness, well, that was a minor god, and Mary worshipped it too. As for ecstasy, Mary favoured the *Penthouse Letters* over the more esoteric guidance in this matter. In her experience, if read out loud, they would arouse any partner. Shy participants didn't need to act out a single uninhibited fantasy. Just the reading of the images led to a satisfying conclusion.

This library dried her out, leaving Mary to argue with herself incessantly, as all the little tornadoes in all the self-help books whirled around, pulling her into their suggested problems and answers. Mary just wanted to like men again.

'Mary, I want to play cards. You deal.' An eight-year-old male had just asked too much as he jumped down the stairs looking for company.

'You deal. I don't want to do all the work.' There was no compromise left in this babysitter.

He accepted her recalcitrance, and sat down. It was a state of mind he lived with on a daily basis. He also mentioned that he didn't know how to deal.

'How old are you anyway?' Mary asked.

'Eight.'

'Well, it's time you learned.' She was gruff, but her instinct to teach was stronger than her desire to punish this boy for his sex's sins.

'First, shuffling.' She showed him how to use his thumbs to control the cards, and when he caught on, praised his dexterity. They played five-card draw for an hour, without laughs or talk, both sulking in their respective pissed off moods, until Lucy came on. Then her silliness cracked their hard little hearts, and they smiled and pointed at her antics to be sure the other one saw the same thing.

'Do you want me to read you a story before bed?' Mary asked.

'No, I can read it myself.'

'Okay, goodnight.'

Nightlights triggered by dusk filled the town home with knee level light. Mary had to unplug the one in the master bedroom, it was so bright. She bruised herself on the mattress, and the sheets, harsh in their newness, chaffed her skin. The little boy slept while Mary tried to remember eight-year-old frustration.

Being a tomboy was such a misunderstood state. Mary had been one when she was really little. At six she couldn't wait until she joined the boys on the branch of a tree. It wasn't a rejection of girls, it was the absolute adoration of boys and their completely interesting activities. They inventoried baseball cards in neat piles, they preoccupied themselves with things that glowed in the dark, and they spent time outside moving fast. It wasn't that Mary wanted to be one, she just wanted to be with them. They reciprocated as they listened to Mary's stories about Nazis, the then generic term for evil men, like martians or aliens. They admired how she oiled her mitt, neatly like a girl, but backed up with a strong throwing arm. They wanted her to sleep over and show her their collections of dinosaurs and minerals. Mary and the boys had a profound crush on each other. The only time she escaped from boyness or girlness to become her essential self was when she read. That was something she did alone. Books seemed to be the only place where she could find girls like herself. Stories from England especially told of girls who carried torches and explored caves. Heroines. Of course, that country had a Queen, it made sense.

Tomorrow, Mary would try to be nicer to Christopher. She would have been if they had engaged at all. It was Saturday and he watched TV in his room from 7.30 to lunch, 12.30 to dinner, and 6.00 to bedtime.

'I have a book report due on Monday. I don't know what to do.' He yelled down as he turned off his light.

'I'll help you.' Mary answered, dreading the prospect of getting this kid to actually do anything.

Hours into the next viewing day when Mary suspected there was only news, cooking shows, and grownup sports and movies on television, Christopher yelled down, 'When are we going to do this?'

'Anytime you turn off the set.'

'It's off.'

Mary saw Christopher's work sheet tremble as he showed her the assignment, but she showed him no mercy.

'Come on, it's your homework, not mine. What do you have to do?'

'A mobile.'

'OK, get going.'

'I don't know what a mobile is.' The weight and size of the boy began to shake around a smaller internal self, but he held on for a few more seconds. He sat at his desk trying not to cry. Mary stood in the middle of the room, still unmoved by this child, who in his despair, had abandoned all efforts to be nice or communicate with anyone.

'Didn't the teacher tell you what a mobile is?'

'She asked if we knew, and all the kids said yes. I'm new in the class so I didn't say anything.' Now he really started to shake, but his hands stayed at his sides as the tears literally splashed on the edge of the desk.

Her heart broke open as she filled with tenderness for this boy. She was eight years old with him, prideful and ignorant, hunting for ways to be in the world. Adult Mary sat on his chair, and put her arm around his shoulder, surprised he didn't pull away. Instead, he cried harder as they tucked into each other, now both staring at the purple mimeographed assignment sheet.

'I miss my mom.'

'I know.'

'She didn't kiss me when she said goodbye.' He sobbed with passion.

'Maybe she was nervous because she was getting on an aeroplane.' Mary instinctively explained the oversight, protecting both the mother and the boy from the possibility of not enough love. But the grief was deeper than a forgotten kiss. Mary held him really close now, as he cried out his other worries.

'I hate the new school. Why did she have to go away when I just started? I'm not comfortable in the cafeteria.' He'd absorbed some of the acceptable lingo from the books downstairs, as he tried to express the difficulty of going to a new school and losing Mom simultaneously. Even the town home was unfamiliar to this little fellow who liked routine and the same foods every day. It was a harsh test. Mary thought of all the boys who got shipped to boarding schools when they were six. How they made it to manhood moved her, and she found a voice in herself so soft, so considerate of Christopher's tiniest fears, that the boy hushed.

'Look, sweet boy, here are crayons and paper. All you have to do is make some drawings from the book. Then we'll cut them out and, well, you'll see.'

'What drawings?'

'Things you liked in the book.'

'There was a boat.'

'Good, draw the boat and colour it.'

Christopher cried a little as he worked, but Mary didn't leave his side, her arm resting around his waist. He wanted her there, there was no mistaking it. She'd seen coloured string in his toy box and taught him to make a little hole in the paper by folding it over, and cutting a half moon. He did it perfectly the second time. His hands were not accustomed to craft work. Only his thumbs knew Nintendo, and Mary drew on unexpected reserves of patience as she taught rigid fingers to cut the string and tie a knot.

They were loving the sitting together on the chair, and Mary stretched it out as long as she could, but finally they had to find a hanger in the closet to complete the mobile. The boat was purple, red and orange. Stick figure characters and a diamond baseball field completed the display, and Mary hung it on the arm of a lamp for them to admire.

'That's a mobile.'

'Cool.'

'Do you want to come downstairs and watch TV with me? I think your Mom would let you stay up an extra half hour after all this work.'

'OK.'

Mary put an afghan over both of them on the cold leather sofa in the living room. The last time she'd been on a leather sofa was with Lawrence, trying to keep her secretions off the animal skin. What was it with these leather sofas? They were inhospitable to the max; clammy, noisy, and freezing, like sitting on a slab of ice at the skating rink, but they'd made it to some level of status with the successful, straight, single guys. Mary remembered when Raymond had bought an entirely different kind of sofa to celebrate a monthly high T-cell count. Raymond knew about comfort.

'Mary, get a gun and shoot me. I've gone absolutely bananas.'

'More than normal?'

'$3,000, Mary, $3,000 for a couch. It's on the credit card, so it will cost me four. And I don't care, it's fabulous. It could sleep two. Literally. It's like having a spare room. Come right over.'

'What colour is it?'

'Celadon.'

Mary had to laugh. 'What is Celadon?'

'Bottle-green, like the ocean. But much paler. It also has flecks of burgundy and bronze. And fringe, Mary, all around.'

The fringe threw Mary off. She pictured some contained Victorian piece, and wondered if Raymond really had lost his mind.

'I'll be right over.'

It was the most beautiful sofa Mary had ever seen in her life. Looking at it was like being stoned. To start with it was a huge, completely relaxed 'L'. Two people could lie feet touching at the corner or heads touching, and find a resting place for every extremity on pillows the size of baby elephants. Raymond and Mary settled in toe to toe, so they could see each other while they talked.

'This is incredible. I could live here.'

'I plan to.'

'When you said fringe, I thought prissy, but this just sets off the size and colour. It's totally sensual.'

'And the fabric, Mary. You could have a baby on this fabric. Soft, darling, nothing to hurt our delicate skin.'

In present time, Mary and Christopher sat on Bill's manly sofa finding softness only in each other and the afghan. Mary held the remote, flashing through ninety channels until they glimpsed a huge monster stomping on Tokyo.

'Godzilla!' Mary pointed to the set, more excited than the boy, and he was impressed too. The man in the monster suit walking on obvious miniatures, cut together with footage of people running in a blatantly different setting, was story-telling at its simple best, like the fairy tales or myths.

It was a handleable monster, awesome and destructive but obviously fake. It soothed them both, and when Mothra flew over Tokyo to battle Godzilla, Christopher jumped up with real eight-year-old animation.

'Mary, I've seen this before. At the video arcade. What's his name again?'

'Godzilla.'

'Yes, Godzilla.' Christopher's tongue thrilled at the word. 'Do you know about this? Have you seen this before?'

'My father took me to these movies. There's a whole series. Mothra. Monster Zero. Megalon. Tetra. But Godzilla's the best. Japanese people made these movies. That's why the mouths don't go with the words. It's in a different language, with English dubbed over. See, look at the lips.'

'Oh, yeah. Lipsinc. Is Godzilla American?'

'No, he's Japanese. They invented him.'

'I want to do a mobile on this, with Godzilla and Mothra.'

Mary and Christopher finished out the movie together, this curious bond reinforcing their affection for each other. When she walked him up to his room, he accepted her goodnight kiss, then put his Nintendo-trained arms around her neck and kissed her on the cheek. What lovers these little boys were going to make, with their fingers sensitive to every blip of the Mario Brothers on their hand-held remotes.

· *Thirty* ·

Mary woke up in mid-orgasm. She was back in her own bed, with an old college boyfriend pumping away full throttle in her wet dream. Mary's spasm continued as she tried to orient herself to the adult lust expressing itself in this teenage manner. The words 'when you miss me enough, you'll give it a grab' came back to haunt her as Mary's subconscious took care of her needs. It was some of the best sex she'd ever had.

She really wanted to ignore the possibility that Arthur and Christopher had softened her up for the fathers.

Obviously, there were no dominance games to play with the little ones who needed her so badly. They were easy to love. Nonetheless, some force was rocking Mary on her sublimely comfortable, recycled mattress. She held onto her fantasy man as long as she could. As he faded, he pulled the real ones into her sleepy, resistant mind. Standing lion-hearted, like Jimmy did for her anger, like Lawrence

263

did for her indifference, and like Raymond did with his love.

Mary thought of calling the old boyfriend, but remembered she'd have to talk to him in order to have sex, and he wouldn't leave right after. Instead she called Jane, a new girl she'd seen working in the flower shop at the corner of Western and Franklin.

Jane had that ambivalent look in her eye. She didn't even know it was there, but Mary could spy it at a hundred paces. That and the fragrant hair and tough hands from cutting thousands of thorny stems. Sensuality was the name of the game, and the memory of Lawrence's dry speedy approach confined Mary's lust for a man to her dreams.

'I wish they'd cut tuberoses after they blossom. They really kill the scent when they cut them too soon.'

'It's a big problem,' said Jane. 'But the growers need the money and the space, so I get baby stalks.'

This doesn't get any easier, thought Mary, as she hunted for topics to break the ice. How long do you hold the eye before it becomes apparent that the life story of tuberoses is not the only reason one has come into the store? Raymond would know. 'More than a five count, darling, and they're yours. Five, six, seven, eight, showtime.'

This girl hadn't shifted or blinked in half a minute. But sometimes they were stoned. The eye test wasn't the only gauge.

'I have a little boy. That's why I work here. My husband flaked out. I don't get child support,' Jane offered.

Mmmm. Politically vulnerable. Too young to be part of the feminist wave, but feeling the anger nonetheless. On the other hand, pretty. Mary doubted the presence of a child would cool the pursuit of any number of guys.

'Do you ever date women?' Mary asked the question ambiguously as if it were a long suffering joke. There were lots of flower shops. Mary would never have to see this one again. Her headache would either go directly to embolism and she would die, or she might have a date after work.

'Hah. Well, I've thought about it.' At least this Jane was honest. 'I might be willing to talk about my fantasies, but I don't know if I could really do anything.'

'Well, why don't we go for food later and talk about our fantasies.' They were both smiling now at their mutual bravado.

'I'll have to bring my kid.'

'Of course. We could meet at that coffee shop on Larchmont around seven.'

Mary dressed like a girl, throwing a skirt over her leggings and combat boots. This was definitely a two girl encounter, marked by the thrill of ambivalence. Jane's son was absorbed in his toys and spent most of the time under the table zooming cars around their feet.

'My husband was a mistake,' Jane started. 'I haven't been really serious about anybody except my son since we broke up two years ago. I haven't had time.'

'Everybody's got time.' Mary was speaking for herself as much as Jane. Choice must play some part in the legion of attractive women who weren't dating.

'I know, but with a kid and work, I need someone to help, who isn't expecting a femme fatale every minute.'

They'd gotten into heavy territory too quickly and Mary tried to lighten it up by laying out her heterosexual credentials. This reassured them both as they smelled each other's perfume.

'I just broke up with my boyfriend, but I don't miss him at all. Actually, I miss the sex, but just the sex, not the sex with him.' Mary explained.

Jane leaned under the table to say 'hi' to her son, brushing her hair against Mary's knee. She came up fast, flushed from bending over, perhaps. They drank herb tea, talked about diets and thought about sex. The boy got restless, and when his antics finally forced his mother to get up, Jane looked at Mary pointblank, and said clearly, 'I'm not saying no, but you'd have to do it all,' as the blood came up high in her face again.

Mary walked her to her car, doubting the wisdom of taking full responsibility for this or any other liaison, when Jane gave her the long hug of the sexually aware. She walked with Mary's body, draping herself with female dependency, the bent elbows and head of submission, backed up by the spinal and pelvic strength of aggression.

It was easy to reconcile Jane's passive words with her tensile hug. Promoting desirability with passion before departure was one of the better weapons in any girl's arsenal of seduction. It was the phrase, 'you'd have to do it all', that reminded Mary she didn't want to. Reciprocity had to figure. Mary knew Jane was talking literally and the idea of taking the virgin was too scary. She pictured the lovely but entirely inactive Jane lying immobile, testing herself for response to Mary, whose tendency in first time encounters was to tremble uncontrollably until some reassurance calmed her down. Mary just wasn't man enough.

· *Thirty One* ·

Mary wandered down Larchmont listening to the starlings cry out with end-of-the-world fervour as the sun went down. It was probably some sort of biological signal; the intensified chirping as the sky turned purple, and thousands of living birds demanded she listen to their natural cycle in the middle of the city.

Perhaps Alfred Hitchcock took this moment, so familiar to all the shopkeepers on the block, as the inspiration to twist nature's darlings into a vicious flying enemy in his movie *The Birds*. These were Hollywood creatures after all. The famous sign was visible to anyone looking north.

The health food store was still open, so Mary decided to pick up some oranges. In any other city, the size and glitter of the building would have indicated a supermarket instead of a specialty shop. It was glorious; organic produce in glistening, triangular stacks; at least two lanes, bowling alley length, just for vitamins; two more lanes for the sugarless products, cakes, candy, ice cream, cookies, and jam all sweetened with fruit juice; bins of grains, rices, and pastas grown in fields without insecticide; cheeses, yoghurts and milks made from animals other than the cow; all displayed under non-flourescent light. It was as good as going to the movies. No wonder the store stayed open at night.

Mary saw him before he saw her. The dried fruit salesman was lifting a crate behind a counter at the end of the meat substitute section, an aisle devoted entirely to soy products. He didn't look quite as big as he did on the day he defended her touching of the candy, but he was tall and nice-looking in his white bib apron. He looked like a merchant who might sing and dance in a movie musical, like they did in *Oliver* or *Hello, Dolly*.

Mary was trying to find out what the ingredients were in carob. This seemed more important to her than the salesman, besides a second meeting might mean talk and a conclusion to her fantasy. She walked in the opposite direction toward the checkout counter. There was a long line, and finally, when the customers got restless, the clerk spoke into her microphone, 'Phil, to the front, please. We need you, Phil.' Mary heard a crate drop as the dried fruit salesman stopped what he was doing and walked to the front of the store. He opened another register, and Mary's line moved as a group to his lane. She stood in front of the pine tree resin they called gum, and hoped he'd forgotten the candy incident, letting her fade anonymously into the night. At the same time she liked the shine of his balding forehead. It looked approachable and gentle, exposing his eyes, as they squinted a little with the new task of checking out the groceries.

His fingers and eyes just saw her merchandise, until she handed him a five dollar bill. Then he looked at her and right away said, 'Oh, it's you.'

'Yes, hi.'

His face was the second one to turn red that night as he said, 'Hold on a second, I want to ask you something. Let me just take care of these customers.'

Mary, still in a flush from Jane's hug, was hoping he'd jump over the counter and take her in front of the bottled water, but contained herself. He was, after all, just a substitute. Then again, Jane had been a substitute for her wet dream. The only authentic lover in Mary's life was a shadowy amalgam of high school energy and male parts living in her head while she was asleep.

'I'll be by the magazines.' Mary took her package and walked to the news section devoted to health and fitness publications. She'd been wanting to read up on Black Cohash, the rumoured estrogen replacement used by American Indian women for centuries. Fortified by her hunt for female knowledge, she anticipated his question. There was nothing like Indian lore to intensify the mystery of squaw and brave. Let him be the brave one for a change.

She wondered if his head was throbbing like hers did when she was going to ask out a girl.

Her answer would either cure it instantly or leave it to harden until sleep uncoiled the nervous muscles.

As he brushed back his non-existent hair, and walked toward her, she liked him so much she started to shake. He might as well see the truth about her right away. Instinctively he put his hand on her arm, then took it away again, as he realised he was touching her too soon.

'Are you OK?' he asked.

'Yes. It's just that I don't normally talk to people so much taller than I am.' He took the remark as a compliment as she knew he would. Put a little spin on the truth and you've got flirting.

'Would you like to go to the movies with me some night? That guy hasn't been back to the store since you touched the candy. I'd like to celebrate. Your germs scared him away.'

'You remembered.'

'A small woman standing up to an obvious psychopath. Well, yes.'

'You were the muscle. I think he would have hit me, if you hadn't shown up.'

'Phil, broken glass in Produce. Bring the mop.' The intercom spoke, and Phil's pride from Mary's compliments deflated with the public orders to clean up the mess. Maybe he'd drop his shoe on the way back to Produce, and Mary would have to comb the neighbourhoods to find his perfect foot, while the wicked store manager kept him in the back.

He defended his humiliation with the standard Hollywood line, 'This isn't what I really do.' Every service position in town was filled by illegal aliens or people who wrote, acted, designed, directed, and produced. Mary sometimes wondered if Los Angeles itself wasn't the real show everybody was putting on.

'Phil, to Produce.' The intercom repeated itself, and Mary stopped shaking long enough to write down her phone number. His eyebrows dropped an inch when she gave him the answer he wanted. And his hip cocked with pleasure as she relaxed into her combat boots and told him her name.